NOTORIOUS SOUTHTOWN

The sordid history of south Coffeyville, Oklahoma and the surrounding area

BY
PRESTON HADDAN

Registration Number

TXu 2-431-585

Printed in the United States of America

FORWARD

While growing up as a child in Coffeyville, Kansas, I knew at an early age of a little town south of the Kansas-Oklahoma state line. It was a small, nondescript town we usually bypassed on the new US 169 Highway that had moved approximately two blocks west. There was a restaurant located towards the south end of town called Bones Café. It was an old World War II barracks that was moved from the former army air training base north of Coffeyville. My father loved to go there on Sundays, and the fried chicken was the best around. While waiting for our food, my father would tell stories of South Coffeyville when it was a wild town full of bars and dance halls. To get to Bones Café, we would normally travel down South Coffeyville's main street, which had previously served as US 169. While we traveled down that street, I would vainly search for those bars and dance halls and found none. My father explained that bars had closed when the new highway was built. I accepted his word as gospel and went about growing up and graduating from Field Kindley High School.

It wasn't until I moved back to Coffeyville from Los Angeles in the late 1970s that the old South Coffeyville stories came to my attention. At this time, I was an insurance agent in Coffeyville and decided to get an Oklahoma Insurance license. To me, South Coffeyville, now a bedroom community for Coffeyville, was ripe for an enterprising insurance agent to go after some new business.

During the summer of 1981, I knocked on almost every door in South Coffeyville. While attempting to sell insurance, I heard stories of the town during its notorious heyday. Despite my interest in the stories, I didn't pursue any kind of information gathering or recording. I was naively convinced that someone was gathering the town's history for a publication someday. I was wrong.

My family moved away from Coffeyville in 1987, never to return for any length of time. In 2006, we moved back to Southeast Kansas, and thanks to Facebook, I reconnected with old Coffeyville classmates and friends. Around 2010, several Coffeyville historical Facebook sites appeared, and I joined. During the following years, occasional tales of South Coffeyville would appear, but despite my interest, I continued to believe that someone had documented the town's notorious past.

After 30 years of working in the community college education system, I retired in 2018 and moved to Springfield, Missouri. Despite my move, I remained active in the Facebook Coffeyville historical sites. Around June 2023, a discussion occurred regarding South Coffeyville and its notorious past. I asked everyone involved in the discussion if anyone had recorded the history of the town, and nobody knew. I was disappointed and declared that if there wasn't anyone recording a history of the town, I was going to write it. After a lot of encouragement, I started my research and was shocked that the Oklahoma Historical Society, Bureau of Investigation, US Library of Congress, National Archives and even the Nowata County Historical Society had virtually nothing on South Coffeyville. The South Coffeyville Historical Society had nothing more than a small caption they had cut and pasted from the Oklahoma Historical Society. When I contacted the South Coffeyville City Clerk and told her of my project, she was shocked by the stories I told. She was 44 years old and knew nothing of South Coffeyville's past. I gave her my name and phone number and asked for any old timers who had knowledge of the town's past to call me. It didn't take long to get a call.

Before going any further into my narrative, I want to thank the following people. Most important is Lonnie Lee, my old jogging partner. Lonnie was born in South Coffeyville in 1943 and has an impeccable memory of South Coffeyville during its notorious heyday and afterward. Without Lonnie, this project would have never gotten off the ground. His son, Jason, has also provided a drawing of the crane truck used for the bank heists.

I also want to thank George Elliot and Jack Cody and their impeccable memory of South Coffeyville, and Steve Garner, a Coffeyville native with a love for local history. And lastly, I cannot exclude Ed Todd, a Coffeyville native who gave me some great stories and a blackjack that at one time was owned by Tommy Hill. There are others. Mike Reister, Bobby Owen, and Peggy Little also provided me with valuable information.

TABLE OF CONTENT

Chapter 1
The Origins Of Two Sinful Border Towns And A New State

In 1869, a small settlement was started by Colonel James Coffey, and that same year, it received a post office. Originally, Coffeyville was in competition for a railroad line with another small community called Parker. Probably because Parker was located next to the continuous snaking of the Verdigris River, Coffeyville won the rail contest. Its proximity ran parallel to the Verdigris River and offered a clearer path and fewer bridges to Oklahoma Territory. Soon, Coffeyville became a small, prosperous farming community with rail facilities and merchants who could supply area farmers, including those located south of the Kansas state line. Humorist Will Rogers once stated that as a boy, he would travel with his father to Coffeyville for supplies. This story probably took place in the early 1880s when Tulsa, Bartlesville, and Nowata didn't exist. One can only imagine the time it took for Rogers and his father to travel from Oolagah to Coffeyville.

Coffeyville, located in the southernmost portion of Southeast Kansas, was in many ways a typical eastern Kansas town of the mid-1800s. The people originally located there were mostly white European immigrants who moved to Kansas from the upper states. They were strong, hard-working people who farmed the land to produce wheat and/or corn and raised cattle for local markets. Seizing an opportunity to either get rich or at least make a good living, merchants from other northern states settled in Coffeyville and started highly successful business ventures. With two major regional railroads running through town and a vast area to the south that had no settlements to speak of until the 1890s, Coffeyville was a good place to settle.

However, there will always be a political hitch that can spoil a place that, to many, was considered a land of milk and honey.

Due to a strong temperance movement, led in part by Carrie Nation, Kansas voted to ban liquor in 1880. Although the rest of the state might have felt heavenly and righteous with being the first state in the union to ban all alcohol except for medical purposes, Southeast Kansans knew hypocrisy when they saw it. Mining towns like Pittsburg, Columbus, Galena, and others ignored the new law and readily took advantage of the much looser liquor laws in Missouri. Even Coffeyville, which was about 50 miles west of the Missouri border, was no exception. It, too, ignored Kansas prohibition and brought liquor and beer from Missouri, and also from Oklahoma Territory, where law enforcement barely existed.

Events in Coffeyville took an amazing turn when the Dalton gang, who were considered Coffeyville residents, unsuccessfully tried to rob two banks at the same time in 1892. The Daltons, who lived in Coffeyville, were distant relatives of the James and Younger clans. At various times, the Dalton brothers, except for the youngest, Emmett, were peace officers. Only the oldest, Frank, would remain as a lawman. Bob and Grat got into trouble over an alleged theft of horses and were fired as deputies. Since stealing horses was considered a capital crime at that time, the two brothers decided to embark on a life of crime, robbing banks. They eventually built a gang consisting of outside members and their little brother, Emmett. After a series of bank robberies in Kansas and Oklahoma Territory, the Daltons decided to rob two banks at once in their former hometown of Coffeyville. The date was October 5, 1892, and the robberies did not go well. First, a local citizen recognized the Daltons and their fake beards. Also, Grat had a funny way of sitting on his saddle and was spotted immediately by a local citizen.

As the robberies were in progress, local citizens ran into the Isham Hardware store and grabbed handguns and rifles. They lined up in front of the store giving them a clear line of fire into the alley where the gang had hitched their horses. Bob, the oldest brother in the gang and self-appointed leader, took his youngest brother Emmett and robbed the First National Bank next door to Isham Hardware. The brothers stole a large amount of cash and gold but found their bags so heavy they had trouble making a quick escape to their horses. In the meantime, middle brother Grat and two other members of their gang weren't so lucky robbing the Condon National Bank. The bank employee falsely claimed that the safe couldn't be opened due to a timer on the lock. The ruse forced the three robbers to wait until gunfire from the local citizens forced them to flee without any loot. The three robbers were caught in a narrow alley across from the Isham Hardware Store. This location gave citizens firing from that location a narrow range to shoot. Grat and his accomplices were caught in the deadly corridor of gunfire that mortally wounded all three. Dick Broadwell was able to get on his horse and flee, but he was later found dead at the edge of town. Meanwhile, Bob and Emmett had circled behind both banks and attempted to mount their horses from an adjoining alley. Bob was killed while trying to mount his horse. Emmitt, trying to help his mortally wounded brother on his horse, was seriously wounded from a shotgun blast. By the time the shooting was over, two of the three Daltons and the two other gang members were dead. Only Emmett survived with 22 large buckshot holes in him. Emmitt would later spend the next 15 years in the Kansas State Prison in Lansing.

The gunfight cost Coffeyville four citizens, leaving the town in a state of shock and sadness. The alley where the Dalton Gang met their end became famous as "Death Alley."

From a national standpoint, the Dalton raid was the last of the big bank robberies of the 19th century. From that time on, Coffeyville has been famous as the town that killed the Dalton Gang. To date, three motion pictures and one episode from the "Death Valley Days" television show have been dedicated to the Dalton Raid in Coffeyville. None of these Hollywood productions have accurately depicted the bank robberies and shootouts, but they have kept Coffeyville on the map of old Wild West sites to visit. There is a Dalton Museum in Coffeyville that is now located in the former Condon Bank building across from the first structure that has been restored to its original state. The city's Chamber of Commerce and local historical society hold an annual Dalton raid re-enactment on the October weekend closest to the actual robbery date.

Events changed again for Coffeyville when natural gas and oil were discovered near the town around 1903. Overnight, Coffeyville went from a small farming community to a growing metropolis. Between 1903 and 1910, Coffeyville grew from 4,000 residents to approximately 12,000. The town quickly transformed into an industrial community with electricity, plumbing and sewer services, lighted streets paved in brick from the local brick manufacturers, and public parks. Even a local trolley service was built to serve the community. Local entrepreneurs prospered. Harry Sinclair, a Coffeyville druggist, invested in gas and oil leases and went on to start Sinclair Oil Company, a major US corporation. He would later build a large oil refinery and tank car facility on the north side of Coffeyville close to the Verdigris River. W.P. Brown, another successful local oil and gas entrepreneur, built the beautiful Brown Mansion, a large, three-story home designed by famous New York architect Stanford White. This mansion still exists and is now a community museum, party and wedding venue. In 1911, Brown built the Natatorium. It was a large, two-story regional health spa complete with an outdoor natural springs pool, indoor gymnasium, pool, exercise facilities and doctors available to treat numerous ailments. The Natatorium also featured an amusement park complete with a moat for couples to paddle through. Brown also built a golf course and clubhouse across the street. Since the Natatorium was at the southern edge of town, the local trolley service built a line to it to accommodate visitors from Coffeyville's several train depots. From its inception to the beginning of the "Great Depression" in 1930, the Natatorium was a popular destination point for people seeking a cure for numerous ailments. One of the "cures" that had to be brought in from the outside was illegal liquor.

From the time of the oil and gas discoveries to the beginning of the 1920s, Coffeyville's population grew to over 17,000. It had the Sherwin Williams Smelter that manufactured the oil-based pigment for their paints, two oil refineries, three railroads, a large flour mill, numerous glass factories and even a cigar factory. In addition, downtown Coffeyville had a robust retail sector that served both residential and farming needs up to a 50-mile radius. It was during this period of growth that Coffeyville emerged as a community with two faces. On one side, there was the professional and retail sector that was experiencing financial success and wanted to be considered a "cultured" community. A large, elaborate theater named the Jefferson was built to accommodate local and regional patrons wanting to experience the popular vaudeville and operatic acts traveling across the county at that time. Local literary clubs, a community orchestra, and a new library funded by the Carnegie Foundation became a firm part of the community for those who wanted to consider themselves "cultured.:

On the other side of the community pendulum was the manufacturing sector, which essentially defined Coffeyville as a working man's town. For many years, Coffeyville was referred to as a "lunch pail" town that catered to the factory workers and laborers who consisted of the major population base. Stores had sections dedicated to serving the clothing and other essential home needs of the working sector. One prominent men's clothing store, Strasburgers, had a basement with a section dedicated to clothing for factory workers. Another business named "Old Yellow Front" was opened primarily to serve the factory workers, laborers and their families with low-cost merchandise. Other businesses that served all sectors of Coffeyville and the surrounding area followed later.

Another sector that flourished serving factory workers was the low-cost café. These eating establishments were spartan and served simple, inexpensive meals. Some of the businesses were large enough to house dance halls for workers to let some steam off after a hard day in a factory. These places were usually located on South Walnut, but some were also on Santa Fe Street and other locations scattered at the edge of the South, West, and Eastern parts of town. Some were located discreetly, and others were plainly displayed for all to see. The local police, although available to quell fights and other disturbances, mainly stayed in the background, understanding that the local workforce needed places for entertainment and even an occasional fight or two. As time passed, Coffeyville developed a reputation as a town that preferred to fight with its fists.

Another sector that started early during Coffeyville's industrial expansion was the growth of a large Black population. With glass and brick factories flourishing, Coffeyville needed laborers for those plants and other services that catered to a growing community. Coffeyville's industrial and business growth called for increased demand for laborers, servants, janitors, and domestic employees. Although other towns like Independence, Parsons, and Chanute developed small Black communities, none had the numbers of Coffeyville. The Black population in Coffeyville ranged between 15 to 20% of the entire community, more than double the minority population of any other Southeast Kansas community.

From their arrival, Blacks settled in two areas. The smaller Black sector settled along 12th Street parallel to the east/west Missouri Pacific Railroad tracks. This enclave consisted of Blacks who considered themselves to have the better jobs available to minorities. They were the janitors who kept downtown Coffeyville clean. Some were hired as servants for wealthy Whites. Their wives usually had cleaning, washing and maid jobs. The homes in this area were clean and neat, and they prided themselves as the "better Blacks" of Coffeyville. This sector also had its own businesses along 12th Street. Their numbers were small but helped supply the Blacks in this area with their essential needs. For entertainment, they occupied the second floor of several 11th Street buildings. A recently discovered news article tells of Blacks gambling on West 11th Street. The location is not known, but another tale has emerged that there were several Black drinking establishments on West 12th.

On the east side of Coffeyville was the larger Black community. Some recently discovered stories named this area Dodds City. Unfortunately, this information has not been verified and may have been a name that someone created to identify a person or family who lived there. There have been many names associated with the northeast side of town. Many were racist terms that were common during the pre-civil rights era. In terms of politics, the northeast side of town was the First Voting District of Coffeyville, and its inhabitants considered themselves a political force who could not be ignored. It was located east of the Santa Fe and MKT (KATY) railroad tracks. Its northern border was the Ozark Refinery and Seventh Street. Blacks had their own elementary school, and since they were not allowed during the first half of the 20th century to shop in the downtown sector, segregated businesses opened on the "east side of town." Along with these businesses, something else emerged: entertainment. Even though liquor, gambling and prostitution were banned statewide, Blacks quickly learned that there was money to be made serving the illicit desires of the local White population. Illegal liquor stores located in homes sprang up. So did gambling dens and other hideouts. One of the more notorious and dangerous gambling venues was pit bull fighting along a discreet area on the south side of the Verdigris River by the Ozark Refinery, located immediately west of the original north/south Kansas US 169 highway. Every Saturday afternoon, when the weather was fair and the land was reasonably dry, pit bullfights would be held. The fights would start at Noon and continue until dark, or there was only one dog left. Betting was fierce, and so was each fight until one of the dogs was killed. Complaints over a betting loss could lead to a quick death. Bodies would be dumped into the river, never to be found. The origins and exact details of this activity were not well known for many years and as a result, it was a fairly well-kept secret. However, by the 1980s and partly because of community concerns over the alleged dangers of pit bulls, the dog fighting secret became public knowledge. Even with the secret out, there are rumors to this day that the pit bull fights by the Verdigris River continue.

Another gambling venue was cock fighting behind homes protected by makeshift fences. There were two areas of cock fighting in Coffeyville. The first was in the southern part of Coffeyville, known as "fish worm flats." This part of town, initially settled by glass manufacturing employees, had a culture of its own. The citizens there considered themselves independent from the rest of Coffeyville. They bred and raised pit bulls, had their own bars, and conducted cock fighting behind several doors.

Cock fighting also took place in the Black area of East Coffeyville. These fights mostly catered to the Blacks who lived there and were rumored to be quite lively with drinking and dancing after the fights. Coffeyville police knew about the pit bull and cock fights but chose to ignore them and avoid any unnecessary racial tension.

During the first half of the 20th century, Race relations between Blacks and Whites in Coffeyville were tentative at best, and it did not take much for a White person to quickly anger a Black with racist comments. This level of animosity was also evident in the rest of Montgomery County and Southtown. Despite the animosity, Whites wanting cheap sex would readily travel to the Black end of town to take advantage of the prostitution available there. However, there were homes, mostly shacks, that provided prostitutes. The most popular was the two-story "rooming house" on East Martin Street that was the main Black prostitution house in Coffeyville. It was a large wood frame building with a small front entrance. Customers would enter, and in front of the stairway and lower hallway was a small booth where a customer would tell what kind of service he wanted and the amount he was willing to pay. The customer was escorted into a small living area and shown who was available. There were six rooms on the first floor and eight on the second, with rear exit doors on both floors. The only time the Coffeyville police would show up was when a fight would break out. This location, which survived into the 1970s, served both Blacks and Whites. It was in a secluded part of town and mostly unknown to the White community, except for its customers. The rooming house also served as the "go-to" place for teenage boys looking to lose their virginity.

The Black community, despite its notorious reputation, could not be a stand-alone enterprise in the days of segregation and third-class citizenship for practically all Blacks. Without the blessing of White community leaders of Coffeyville and later South Coffeyville, illicit activities there would have had difficulty existing. In the beginning, Southtown was a primary supplier of illegal liquor and beer to the east side of Coffeyville. However, as time passed, the Black community would begin its own brewing and moonshine production. Even though Blacks preferred to be the masters of the vices in their area, their leadership knew well that they needed the "silent" blessing of White leaders to ensure at least some level of autonomy. The Black community also knew that their activity west of the KATY and Santa Fe railroad tracks needed to be severely limited. The US Supreme Court ruled in the Plessy vs. Ferguson Decision in 1896 that segregation in the entire country was the law of the land. Essentially, Whites would dictate the lives of Blacks throughout most of the country with strict segregation laws and voter suppression and keep them in small, segregated clusters away from White businesses, jobs, schools and neighborhoods. Coffeyville was no exception to the rule, and its White citizens went to great lengths to keep Blacks east of the railroad tracks and south of 11th Street. In South Coffeyville, there were no racial boundary lines, but stories from older residents indicate that Blacks were not allowed to roam freely in the city or have access to the numerous bars there.

Whether a person was White, Black or any other race, it was very clear early on in the city's history that Coffeyville was going to march to its own drum in terms of politics and social issues. It was going to take care of its own business despite the prudish rulings from Topeka. With this kind of modus operandi in mind, it was the new state of Oklahoma and later South Coffeyville that came into the picture and gave liquor and gambling a life of its own.

CHAPTER 2
EARLY HISTORY OF OKLAHOMA

In 1874, the US Army engaged the Southern Cheyenne, Comanche, and Arapaho tribes in what was called the "Red River War." The participating tribes lost and were forced to settle in Southern Oklahoma, thus forever ending their previous livelihood. The next major action in Indian Territory was the 1889 Oklahoma Land Rush that took place in the north central part of Oklahoma and consisted of land that had been previously allotted to the Creek and Seminole peoples. This event, which poured thousands of White settlers into Native American lands, was the foundation of the creation of Oklahoma Territory under the Organic Act of 1890. Even though the territory tribes attempted to create their own state with the Sequoyah Convention Constitution in 1906, they were refused by the US government. Under the Organic Act, two territories were formed: The Oklahoma and Indian Territories. This act also became the foundation for statehood in 1907. The Organic Act also segregated alcohol sales and consumption. The sale and distribution were legal in Oklahoma Territory (mostly western Oklahoma) but illegal in Indian Territory. Essentially, Northeast Oklahoma, which was part of the Indian Territory, was legally dry from 1890 to 1959.

When statehood was granted to Oklahoma in 1907, the Native-American tribes were incorporated into the state. Much of what had been land designated to the indigenous tribes there was essentially opened to white settlers to purchase and settle. By the time Oklahoma joined the union, white settlers were growing in numbers as more land opened. Even though the white population would ultimately dominate Oklahoma society, the state never lost its Native American influence. Indigenous schools, tribal councils, clinics and hospitals proliferated and to this day continue to influence Oklahoma culture greatly. But, back to the story of Oklahoma's liquor laws and how they influenced the founding of South Coffeyville and the true reason for its existence.

When Oklahoma entered the union in 1907, one of its first major pieces of legislation and constitutional measure was the complete ban on the making, selling, distributing, and consumption of alcoholic beverages. One of the bad jokes from Whites was Native Americans could not handle "fire water." When drunk, they would become wild and dangerous. Therefore, White legislators and other elected officials felt it necessary to keep liquor away from "Indians." Oklahoma joined the union in the middle of a spreading nationwide temperance movement. Kansas, a state that had supposedly been dry since 1880, directly north, didn't help. Whether it was the temperance movement or a desire to keep liquor away from Native Americans, the result was a statewide ban on liquor in 1907. Thus, Oklahoma joined Kansas as a dry state.

SOUTH COFFEYVILLE AND ITS ORIGINS

Even before South Coffeyville became a community, enterprising men who settled into Nowata County quickly learned that Coffeyville and its rapidly growing industrial base had a serious thirst for liquor, gambling and other vices. Many of Coffeyville's new residents moved there to work in the factories and came from northern states where liquor was legal and gambling, although illegal, flourished. Until nationwide prohibition went into effect, Missouri, as a state with rather lax liquor laws, became a major supplier of bootleg liquor and beer. As roads developed in Missouri, "roadhouses" opened along them. These establishments provided liquor, dancing, and other forms of entertainment. These roadhouses, along with legal liquor distributors in towns like Springfield and Joplin, would serve as the suppliers for Oklahoma bootleggers.

The early bootleggers were men who saw an opportunity to make money and to take care of a demand situated north of the Oklahoma line. All they had to do was ~~to~~ make the trek by horse drawn wagon to either Joplin, but mainly Springfield, for their bootleg supplies. Once the bootleggers reached their destination in Missouri, they would then have to take a path free of federal marshals to reach Oklahoma. The federally funded Lake of the Cherokees, better known for its large size as Grand Lake in Northeast Oklahoma, would not be constructed until 1940, leaving that part of the state open to travel overland. Once in Oklahoma, the bootleggers had a choice of growing communities to serve. There were Miami and Vinita, communities that would readily welcome illegal liquor for their citizens. However, the prize was Coffeyville. It was by far the largest and fastest-growing town and less than a mile north of the Oklahoma border. However, there was one problem. The closest Oklahoma town to Coffeyville was Nowata and it was over 20 miles away. In 1908, that distance could amount to a half day of travel one way, especially considering Oklahoma roads (if any) and their condition. The only logical answer was to start a town just south of the Kansas border with easy access to Coffeyville.

Around 1903, the time Coffeyville was in the beginning of its industrial boom, a small unincorporated cluster of homes started to appear just south of Coffeyville and the Kansas/Oklahoma border. Other little settlement clusters in the area also appeared. One was a KATY loading dock called Noxie, located about five miles east. However, it was the settlement just south of Coffeyville that caught on as a place to settle and build. Coffeyville businessmen quickly noticed the little settlement south of the state line and decided it would be a great location for a new community. So, in 1909, the community of South Coffeyville, Oklahoma, was incorporated, and a post office was established soon after. At its inception, the town had a population of 196, with John P. Etchen as one of its prominent citizens.

From its humble beginnings, South Coffeyville had the makings of a town with a future. It had two railroads running through or just outside it, the Missouri Pacific and the KATY. At its inception, South Coffeyville was a heavily promoted town trying to attract families, businesses and even industry. Articles from the South Coffeyville and Lenapah newspapers indicate that the new community was promoted as an Oklahoma extension of Coffeyville. In a 1909 copy of the South Coffeyville Times, a large promotion advertisement was dedicated to promoting the town. An architect's drawing of a new brick two-story school was displayed, as well as a map of the town. The map was unique in that it displayed the two current railroad lines plus an extension line being considered by the Santa Fe Railroad to run parallel to the KATY line to South Coffeyville, providing that a brick plant would be located there. There were also early plans to build two railroad depots but would later be reduced to one serving both lines. It would be called Union Station. The station, completed by 1912, was located where the two railroads intersected. By 1912, the SEK Interurban, which started in Nowata and ran through Coffeyville to Parsons, Kansas, was completed and had tracks and a trolley stop right in the middle of town. South Coffeyville also had a direct road that led to South Willow 5Street in Coffeyville. If Southtown had a disadvantage, it was the fact that it did not have a direct east-west route to anywhere. Later, that lack of an east/west route would prove advantageous to robbers and gangsters.

Despite all of the promotional efforts, South Coffeyville never materialized as an Oklahoma extension of Coffeyville. One major problem was the fact that the Verdigris River and Onion Creek were prone to flooding. South Coffeyville had a high enough elevation that kept it from being flooded. However, Coffeyville was not so fortunate. Until a levy was built many years later, the east and southern portions of Coffeyville flooded every 10 to 15 years. Early maps of Coffeyville clearly show streets stretching to Onion Creek. An electric power plant is shown to have been considered just south of the Natatorium. The plans looked promising except the southern development and proposed power plant would have been built on a flood plain. After several early floods, these plans were eventually discarded. So, thanks to an unfortunate floodplain, Coffeyville and its new southern neighborhood never connected.

Even before South Coffeyville became incorporated, prohibition in both Kansas and Oklahoma would, unfortunately, prevent the town from reaching the goals its original leaders had planned. As early as 1904, South Coffeyville was developing a reputation as a haven for hooligans and troublemakers. These individuals of questionable character quickly found South Coffeyville as the perfect place to hide from the law. They could cross into Kansas, create mayhem and then quickly slip back into South Coffeyville while Kansas peace officers would not be allowed to cross the state line. Another problem that quickly arose was the small collection of shacks that would serve bootleg liquor and, where room allowed, offer gambling tables. By the time the town was incorporated, the people of South Coffeyville were beginning to see the real and notorious purpose of their community. They were not going to be able to connect and/or compete with Coffeyville in terms of population and commerce. Coffeyville was simply too advanced, and the flooding issue nullified any plans to connect the two communities. Essentially, South Coffeyville would have to rely on liquor, gambling, and other vices to survive.

Even in the early days of South Coffeyville, the residents there were enterprising enough to see they had something Coffeyville didn't have and that something could be used to their advantage. They were situated in a new state with little or no law enforcement. Nowata County was more concerned with keeping the peace within its own city boundaries and immediate surroundings. To the county sheriff, South Coffeyville was a hole-in-the-wall town that was 25 miles away, and there were no decent roads to travel there. The State of Oklahoma was no better off. It had no state police or any other kind of law enforcement available to patrol the new state. The Oklahoma State Bureau of Investigation would not be formed until 1929, and the Oklahoma State Highway Patrol was another eleven years away. Oklahoma was still relying on federal marshals to maintain some sort of order. In addition, with a new state and no road infrastructure, these marshals had to travel on horseback through open territory. Essentially, South Coffeyville was on its own, and its citizens knew they pretty much had free reign to do as they pleased. Even though the local newspapers began covering illegal activity in the town several years before the town was incorporated, nothing was done to stop the criminals. Kansas couldn't do anything (at this time), and federal marshals were more concerned with other activities. Prior to Oklahoma becoming a new state, the territory was untamed and a perfect place for criminals to hide. Federal marshals, like Bass Reeves, would spend a lot of their time in Oklahoma Territory chasing criminals who thought they had found a haven. Chasing criminals going in and out of Oklahoma would keep these marshals very busy until the late 1930s. With federal marshals occupied elsewhere and having considerable freedom of action without consequences, South Coffeyville entrepreneurs took advantage of the situation and started to look for the best ways to make money. It didn't take them long.

Almost as soon as South Coffeyville came into being, shacks serving as saloons appeared. With illegal liquor and beer coming from Missouri and local whiskey stills, the people of Coffeyville finally had a place to get a drink and not to worry about archaic Kansas laws. Gambling and prostitution soon followed. One enterprising saloon owner went as far as setting up a boxing ring for weekend entertainment. For people traveling through town, a small hotel was built almost as soon as the town began. For better or worse, the dye for South Coffeyville was cast. For the rest of this book, South

Coffeyville will be referred to as "Southtown," a term given to it so long ago that nobody remembers when the reference started.

It only took four or five years for the town to realize that it was not going to be another Coffeyville. The town was quickly establishing itself as a place for entertainment for Coffeyville citizens who didn't want to risk being caught in their hometown or by state liquor and vice enforcers. They would cross into Oklahoma, have their fun and then return without being caught. Southtown would also serve as a refuge for Kansas citizens on the run. Until 1934, Kansas law enforcement agencies could not legally cross a state line to pursue a criminal. Southtown was positioned to become the entertainment haven for Coffeyville.

People from Coffeyville had money to spend but illicit entertainment on the Kansas side had its risks. Even though Coffeyville law enforcement was selective and illegal entertainment was readily available, many of its residents didn't want their vices open to local scrutiny. They wanted the kind of discretion only available in Oklahoma.

Even though bootleg liquor, beer, and gambling were offered throughout Southtown, prostitution began to show itself quickly. Prostitution had been plainly evident in Coffeyville since its inception, with prostitutes clearly displaying themselves in downtown establishments, such as the Alvin and Mecca hotels and the second floor of the building that would later become the Long Bell Hardware store. There was a balcony on the second floor of that building facing Walnut, and on Friday and Saturday evenings, the busiest time for downtown Coffeyville, prostitutes would openly display themselves and their availability. Had prohibition not been in effect in Kansas, Coffeyville could have easily gone the way of Southtown. South Walnut became Coffeyville's entertainment district, but it would never reach the level of debauchery of that little Sodom and Gomorrah south of the state line.

By 1912, Southtown had become the "go-to" place for drinking, gambling, and prostitution. Coffeyville citizens could cross the state line, entertain themselves and then cross again with little worry of being exposed.

Southtown would also find another form of revenue, hiding criminals. With no law enforcement to arrest them, criminals quickly found Southtown as a safe place to hide.

Since the early days of Southtown, evidence of everything that occurred there is now mostly told through handed-down tales and stories by sons and grandsons of former residents. Exact information of the 1904 to 1920 era is limited. Fortunately, there were newspapers in Southtown and a neighboring community, Lenapah, that recorded a lot of the early activities of the community. There are also several excellent sources of information passed down to surviving family members. The first comes from Newton (Newt) R Haddan. During his senior years, Newt would share numerous stories about the early days of Southtown. Newt lived until he was 95 and passed away in 1978. He was a person with a keen memory that stayed with him until his death. Of course, people will sometimes add flavor to their stories to make them sound more interesting, but what impressed his family members most was the consistency of Newt's stories. Newt never deviated from what he told, leading family members to believe that his stories contained a considerable amount of truth. As a result, the stories Newt told about the activities he and his brother, Art, experienced during the early days of Southtown are included in this book.

Born in Nebraska, Newt was one of five children who included a pair of sisters and three brothers, Art, Harry and Carl Haddan. The Haddan family moved to Coffeyville in the late 1880s, and the children attended school there. The family was in Coffeyville during the Dalton Raid, but by the time Newt and Art reached the shootout scene, the action was over, and the bodies of the gang had been moved to the city jail.

By the 1890s, portrait photography had advanced to the point that professional cameras were becoming lighter and easier to use. Developing negatives moved from metal plates to a more flexible type of film, making printing pictures a much easier process. Another innovation originated by the Eastman Kodak Company was the small foldout camera that amateurs could easily use by means of roll film. These innovations inspired Newt and Art to pursue a career in professional photography. In the late 1890s, the brothers started a photography business in Peru, Kansas, a small farming community about 20 miles west of Coffeyville. The studio would initially be named Haddan Brother's Photography. This partnership would last until the early 1930's when Art would sell his interest to Newt and move to Oregon. Newt would continue until 1955 when he sold the business to his son Harold. From that time, Haddan Studio would continue until Harold's death in 1987.

Although they had reasonable success in Peru, the oil and gas boom in Coffeyville, which began in 1903, encouraged the brothers to seize an opportunity to be more successful there. They quickly moved back to their former residence and opened a photography studio and camera store in the downtown business sector. Once established, the brother's photography and retail business quickly prospered. Like most prosperous local businessmen, the Haddan brothers became part of the "Coffeyville crowd" who wanted to let their hair down after work and to have a drink and partake in gambling. Although neither brother gambled much or were heavy drinkers, they still enjoyed a couple of drinks and maybe some dominoes before heading back north to Coffeyville. One of the saloons, called the Nut House Club, built an outside boxing ring for weekend fights. It soon became a popular entertainment venue. The fights included not only local boxers but also traveling fighters who fought for a bout purse. From an early age and unlike his more reserved older brother, Newt showed himself to be a scrappy person with a quick temper and fists to match. As a young teen, Newt was working for a farmer who had a mule with a reputation for hurting hired hands trying to handle him. The mule would force the person trying to tend him into a corner and then kick the daylight out of the unsuspecting victim. Newt was aware of the mule's tactics, so when it was his turn to tend the beast, he took a large 2" x 4" board with him. As expected, the mule tried to corner Newt. Being a person with a quick temper, Newt immediately got angry and hit the mule over the head with his board. He continued to hit the mule until the creature went to its knees, screaming. Afterward, the mule never bothered anyone again. Possessing a fierce temper and competitive nature, Newt channeled his violent tendencies into boxing. Newt liked to box and, during his early years, was an excellent amateur boxer. He also enjoyed the bout purse and money thrown into the ring when he won. Newt didn't win every fight, but he later told family members that he won more than he had lost. During one fight (as Newt told many times), he agreed to a fight with a traveling professional boxer who claimed to have never lost a fight. About halfway through the fight, Newt had been peppered with so many jabs that his eyes were starting to close. To keep from losing the fight and the money he would earn, Newt started going for the other boxer's mid-section. Since sit-ups were not usually a part of a boxer's training regimen during the early days of boxing, the professional had a hard time taking the constant pounding to his midsection. By the 14th round, the professional could not leave his corner, giving Newt a technical knockout. Newt loved to brag about the winnings, which also included whatever was thrown into the ring after a fight. The better the fight, the more money would be thrown into the ring. Newt later admitted that the bar owner gave him two steaks to put one over each eye.

It was during this time that Newt noticed a tall lad with piercing eyes and the demeanor of a very determined person who seemed to be taking mental notes. He worked at the club at various jobs including bouncing. Newt also noticed that this young man was good with a blackjack. He had a sister about his age who was occasionally at the club, displaying a similar determined look and taking mental notes of her own. These two young people will later play major roles in the future of Southtown.

Though there were many enterprising individuals who made their living from vice, there was one person who took advantage of South town's new business opportunities but in a dignified manner. His name was Henry Reister.

Henry was born on May 29, 1871, in Albany, Indiana and grew up there. On April 14, 1891, he married Josephine Mary Weber, also from Albany. Henry was a butcher by trade. Like many people originally from Indiana, Southeast Kansas, with its younger but rapidly growing population and jobs created by the regional gas and coal mining boom, became an enticing attraction for Henry and Josephine. In 1906, the Reisters moved to Coffeyville, where he worked for a local butcher. With Coffeyville growing so rapidly at that time, Henry decided he wanted to take advantage of the more open space offered by the newly incorporated South Coffeyville, Oklahoma. By 1911, the Reisters were settled in Southtown. In 1912, a son named George was added to the family. Although Henry could make a decent living as a butcher, he noticed that Southtown was becoming successful in different ways. Instead of the normal commerce that smaller towns possessed, Southtown relied to a large degree on saloons, with illegal liquor, gambling and prostitution. Customers from Coffeyville and surrounding Kansas communities and Nowata, Oklahoma, could utilize the newly constructed interurban trolley to travel to Southtown. By the time the Interurban was completed in 1912, it had run from Nowata to Delaware, Lenapah, Southtown, Coffeyville, Independence, Cherryvale (another industrial community that by 1910 had a population of over 9,000), and Parsons, a regional train hub for the KATY Railroad. The Interurban had low fares for customers and, by virtue of its track location, served almost every town of any size in Nowata County and Southeast Kansas' Montgomery and Labette Counties. Southtown was in the middle of it with its own trolley stop. People from these Oklahoma and Kansas communities had easy access to Southtown, and Henry took notice.

Being a person with a strong connection to the community he lived in, Henry wanted to prosper with it, but not by selling bootleg liquor at a bar or cheating local suckers with rigged poker games or prostitution. Henry found another avenue to be successful. While traveling from Indiana to Coffeyville, Henry quickly noticed that Missouri, with its strong southern heritage and somewhat hillbilly practices, readily accepted vices such as local poker games and, better yet, locally distilled moonshine. In Missouri, moonshine was popularly titled "hooch." Hooch, whether it was distilled legally or otherwise, was plentiful in Missouri. Springfield, situated in the southern/central part of Missouri and the regional location for federal courts and other government agencies for that era, was right in the middle of what was popularly called the "Ozarks." It was also becoming a regional tourist attraction. In 1913, Lake Taneycomo was formed by damming the James River, and it became a regional destination for early vacationers. Towns like Branson and Hollister quickly grew to accommodate these early vacationers. With this activity and growth as a major location for stone excavation, Springfield also grew as a regional train and retail hub. Along with this progress came a growing thirst for regional liquor, including hooch and bathtub beer. It wasn't until 1921 that prohibition began, and Missouri would prove to be a very reluctant participant.

It was during one of his trips through Springfield that Henry noticed that liquor was easy to acquire but difficult to ship to dry Kansas and Oklahoma. Once established in Southtown, Henry noticed that local distillers could not keep up with demand. As a result, Henry devised a plan to travel to Springfield and return with barrels of bootleg liquor and beer. It was a great plan but not so easy to implement. By 1910, roads from Southtown barely existed. To reach Missouri, Henry had to travel from Coffeyville to Joplin and then find a road that led to Springfield. That was the easy part. The hard part was getting back to Southtown with illegal booze and beer. Henry could get to Joplin easily enough but then would have to travel south to Seneca and then through what was still considered Indian Territory. Once in Oklahoma, Henry could pick routes through that area that would keep him out of the curious eyes of locals who wanted to know what he was hauling. Henry picked his routes well, staying away from new communities like Vinita, Afton, Grove, and Welch. Henry was never caught, demonstrating the great care he took traveling through Oklahoma to Southtown. After a week of traveling, Henry would reach Southtown and serve as a distributor of the goods he brought with him.

By the mid-teens, Henry, along with several other enterprising bootleggers, was keeping a steady supply of illegal liquor and beer coming from Missouri. Local whiskey stills were also emerging around Nowata County without any concern for state laws or local enforcement. When supplies from Missouri were close to being exhausted, Henry would tap local distillers for the liquor needed to keep the handful of local bars open until he could make a round trip to Springfield and back.

A third person who was well-known during Southtown's early years and considered a colorful person was George White Cloud. Around the Southtown locals and area customers, George used only White as his last name. But everyone who was a friend or acquaintance of George concluded that he was a full-blooded Delaware or Osage Native American. George was a large man at six foot five inches and weight well over 200 pounds. He was a very strong man and not a person to antagonize. There were rumors that he once worked for Buffalo Bill's traveling show and wrestled bears. On the other hand, most people found George to be a person with a great sense of humor. For the local saloon owners, George was the unofficial town marshal. During the busiest drinking and gambling hours in Southtown, George could be found somewhere on Main Street taking a nap or nursing a bottle of moonshine. No matter how drunk he was, George readily availed himself to any bar owner who needed some help with an unruly customer or sore gambling loser. George, with his large hands and great strength, could quickly tame any troublemaker. On one occasion, George found himself in the middle of a fight between a bouncer and several drunks with knives pulled. George walked up to the larger of the two drunks and decked him before he knew what happened. The second drunk quickly sobered up and helped his unconscious friend out of the bar. For his efforts, George received $10 and a bottle of moonshine. Unfortunately, George's time in Southtown was short. On a hot Saturday evening, shortly before the United States declared war on Germany and the Kaiser, George was found dead, sitting in his favorite spot. His heart had given out, and he quietly died in his sleep.

It was about this time that the “Whiskey Trail” from Southtown to Coffeyville began. By the mid-teens, Coffeyville’s population had stabilized at a little over 17,000, with many of these new residents factory workers from northern “wet” states who wanted to have a beer or drink after work or on the weekends. In Coffeyville, the glass, tile, and brick plants were operating to capacity to meet regional customer’s needs. Coffeyville was in the process of paving its streets, sidewalks and downtown alley. Other towns, like Caney and Independence, were also paved with brick from Coffeyville. In addition, the downtown merchants had firmly established themselves as the retail sector for customers in a 50-mile radius. This success led to the obvious desire for liquor and entertainment of a dubious nature. Southtown was the normal place of choice for drinking, gambling, and prostitution. It was south of the Kansas state line and far enough away for those who wanted discretion and some privacy. However, not every Coffeyville resident wanted to party in ramshackle dives. There were many who preferred to stay in town and risk getting caught. However, being caught by local police officers was not very likely because from its early days, Coffeyville was lax on law enforcement.

Police departments that originated at the turn of the 19th century were a mixed lot. Some had cars and motorcycles to patrol the town. Others still relied on horses for patrolling. The officers of this early period were poorly trained and usually hired for their toughness and ability to use a gun when needed. Early police officers were also poorly paid; thus, they often looked for other means of income. Coffeyville was no exception. Its city leaders, the downtown merchants and successful local entrepreneurs were more concerned with economic growth and less about law enforcement. Policemen were hired to maintain local peace, not play investigator and harass people over unpopular laws initiated in Topeka. The local philosophy was to arrest those who were obvious thieves or people who liked to damage property. But there wasn't much concern over the vices of South Walnut or other parts of town. People wanted access to their vices and local police officers were willing to accommodate, but at a price. The best way for a local police officer to augment his income was to collect from drinking establishments or individuals who sold liquor, allowed gambling or supported prostitution. With this kind of lax but potentially lucrative enforcement, the reputation of South Walnut in Coffeyville and its vices were solidified.

When Coffeyville became a town and started to grow, the core of the town was the central park area north of 9th street and straddled by Walnut and Union. For many years, this was the central hub of Coffeyville. Even President Taft, who visited Coffeyville, spoke to the residents in this square. But, if Coffeyville had a weakness, it was that there wasn't a true north-south route out of town. If a person wanted to travel north, he would go east on 8th Street to Sunflower on the far east part of town to head north. Traveling South was another story. Willow was the main road south but was located two blocks west of the town's downtown core. To correct that problem, 12th Street became the east/west route for two blocks to Walnut, a street that led directly to the downtown core. Since Walnut was the main route for four blocks, it was this little section of street that became Coffeyville's Road of Sin. It was on Walnut that secret places to drink were established. As stated earlier, in the early teens, the Mecca Hotel was built on the corner of 10th and Walnut. It was the nicest hotel in Coffeyville at the time and the place where travelers would stay before moving on. While in town, they would want to drink and gamble. Rooms would be set up for discreet drinking and gambling. When other vices were wanted, there was a prostitution establishment on the second floor of the large implement store across the street from the hotel.

Because South Walnut had by then become known as the Sodom and Gomorrah of the community, "upstanding" local citizens would avoid it, expecting the local police to contain the sin of the city. However, what the local police did was contain the street and the "Whiskey Trail" from Southtown intact; thus, liquor and prostitution thrived. Newt Haddan once told a story, one of many of his youthful days, that Coffeyville never really cared about the law, and the police were there mainly to keep things from getting out of hand. The town averaged between 12 to sixteen full-time police officers and, by the early teens, had purchased four police cars and three motorcycles. The police department also shared a panel truck with the local fire department for times when it was needed to bring a large number of drunks to the city jail. But, if the illicit activities were peaceful, the police would keep their distance, but for a price. The bars on Walnut Street and along the railroad tracks were expected to pay a regular "service" fee to avoid being raided.

As the teens wore on, life in Southtown and Coffeyville pretty much stayed the same. The Whiskey was flowing from Missouri and local stills. Gambling continued to be available, and prostitution discreetly flourished on both sides of the state line. World War I and the many young men leaving to serve in the army caused business to slow but never to stop.

Fortunately, for Southtown and the Whiskey Trail, the United States didn't enter the war until 1917, and troop mobilization lasted little more than one year.

Just as business was beginning to return to normal, the Spanish Flu, which began in 1919, hit the Coffeyville area and lasted well into 1920. Many children and adults were infected causing Coffeyville and Southtown to slow to a crawl to avoid spreading the disease. By the time the flu had passed, many families in both towns had lost family members. For a brief time, Southtown was quiet as families grieved, but by 1921, the city and all its vices were back in business again.

CHAPTER 3
PROHIBITION AND THE ERA OF TOMMY HILL BEGINS

It is this era that would, for almost 40 years, identify Southtown as the sin city of Northeast Oklahoma and intertwine itself with its larger neighbor north of the state line for many years to come. It was during the beginning of the "roaring 20s" that a particular individual would emerge and establish himself as its principal overlord. That person was Ivan Thomas Hill, better known as Tommy Hill.

On August 21, 1895, Tommy Hill was born in Mound Valley, Kansas. His parents were Franklin and Mabel Hill, and they were farmers. The strong infant would soon be referred to as "Tommy" and nothing else. He followed an older sister born a year earlier, in 1894. Her name was Margorie Perl Hill. From an early age, Margerie would be referred to as Madge. Madge, like Tommy, was smart, and both were enterprising children. Tommy was the boisterous one who liked a challenge. Madge, on the other hand, was more reserved. She was a problem solver and, unlike her younger brother preferred to stay behind the scenes and excel without fanfare. In 1905, a younger brother, Claude S Hill, was born. He would eventually become known as Sandy. Like his older sister, Sandy preferred to excel without any fanfare.

As Oklahoma approached statehood in 1906, the Hills decided to move to an area in Oklahoma south of Coffeyville. The land was cheap and plentiful, and better yet, there was talk of a town starting on the Oklahoma side. In 1907, Oklahoma became the 46th state, and two years later, South Coffeyville, later known as Southtown, was incorporated. The town quickly opened a post office and built a two-story hotel and school. The school was small but was made of brick that was cheap and plentiful from the brick factories located in Coffeyville. In the beginning, the school taught grades one through twelve. The number of students was small, but the education was more than adequate for the period. Graduating students who applied themselves could go into the world with a solid knowledge of math, reading and writing. By 1912, Madge had demonstrated a keen intelligence and a strong aptitude for math. Tommy, who graduated a year later, was a tall, strapping young man who liked his sister, was good in math and demonstrated a knack for organizing activities with himself as the leader. Tommy was also a very good fighter, capable of defeating anyone his size and, in some cases, much larger. Tommy was an ornery young man who enjoyed pushing the limits of what was considered legal and appropriate for the era.

When he graduated from high school, Tommy started working at the local bars, doing whatever was asked of him, whether it was legal or not. The main bar where Tommy worked was the Nut House Club. It was a dive with a bar, limited seating and several tables available for poker. The bar was little more than a glorified shack and much like the other bars located in Southtown during the teens. The normal list of refreshments consisted of illegal whiskey, moonshine and warm beer. In this environment, Tommy flourished. His mathematical skills and ability to keep track of the liquor and beer inventory in his head made him greatly appreciated by the bar's owner. Because of his lean but muscular build, Tommy also served as a bouncer. On one occasion, Tommy confronted a drunk customer much larger than he and, with one punch, had the man on the deck and ready to be dragged to the street. Even though Tommy had a knockout punch, his weapon of choice was the blackjack, a leather baton filled with lead pellets. One rap on the head with this weapon would normally render the receiver unconscious. Made of wrapped leather, much like a whip, Tommy's blackjack looked like something a Native American might have made. After being hidden by Ed Todd, a retired Coffeyville native for over 70 years, the weapon was recently presented to the author and is pictured in this book.

Tommy was good with the blackjack, and the customers who knew him kept their distance. On another occasion, a man from Coffeyville with a reputation for being a tough fighter visited the Nut House Club and made it known that he was a tough person and should be left alone. As the evening wore on, the liquor turned him into a noisy and boisterous drunk. Tommy finally had his fill of this loudmouth and gave him a rap with his blackjack. The man immediately crumpled, giving Tommy the joy of dragging him out of the bar. Because of episodes like this, Tommy was, by his early twenties, a man reputed to be feared by anyone who crossed him. This reputation would stay with Tommy for the rest of his life.

Gambling, despite its popularity, was not an activity that Tommy engaged in. He quickly noticed how crooked the tables were and the amount of money a sucker could lose in one night. So, instead of playing, Tommy decided that the man who controlled the tables and betting odds was where the real money could be made.

Prostitution, consisting mainly of young women, was available in Southtown. Most of these girls were either runaways from home or tramps looking for a place with a bed and the opportunity to make some money. Some earned their keep by flirting and getting men to drink and gamble. Others were prostitutes who discreetly whisked men off to nearby shacks for paid sex. Although prostitution in both Coffeyville and Southtown was mostly kept secret, it was an obvious service that many young men took advantage of. Until the 1960s, men and women lived in an era when a young single woman normally abstained from sex until she was married. A young woman caught in a pre-marital sexual relationship often suffered serious consequences. She was labeled a whore and avoided by almost all eligible bachelors. If that wasn't enough, getting pregnant out of wedlock was even worse. Birth control, outside of condoms, was virtually non-existent. If a single woman became pregnant, she would have to leave town and either live with distant family members or reside in state-run homes for young pregnant women. In most cases, the fatherless child would be adopted by couples unable to have children. The woman would never be able to return home.

With those kinds of consequences, most young women normally abstained, leaving men to seek sexual gratification elsewhere, mainly with prostitutes. Both Coffeyville and Southtown maintained brothels for those young men who wanted sex. Although Coffeyville had several brothels located downtown and in the Black section, it was Southtown that was the most popular and discreet. Men could travel South Willow to Southtown, pick their entertainment venue of choice, and head back to Coffeyville without ever being caught. After all, what God-fearing Christian man or woman would venture to such a lurid den of sin south of the Kansas border?

HIDING CRIMINALS IN SOUTHTOWN

As the Teens progressed, another activity began, which would later be a prominent part of the Southtown culture: hiding criminals on the run. Because of its location just south of Coffeyville, on the state line, and being in the part of northeast Oklahoma where law enforcement barely existed, Southtown was a prime location to hide criminals until the "heat" was off. There was only one true north/south road and none going east/west. To the east was the Verdigris River, which snaked its way south and was a waterway that was difficult to cross by horse. Bridges had only started to be built and were still few and far between. To the west was open land and rolling hills and no water to speak of. A person traveling in that direction would need plenty of food and water or risk dying on the prairie.

Henry Reister, the enterprising bootlegger who later became the Mayor of South Coffeyville, lived outside the city limits and found he could make an easy five dollars a day hiding criminals on the run. Most of the criminals he hid were small-town thugs on the run for horse stealing or maybe a store robbery. Some were more serious criminals who had robbed a bank or killed someone. Most were trying to avoid a federal marshal who had a warrant for one or more crimes committed. Henry and his wife didn't care as long as the person they were hiding behaved themselves. The food cellar was usually the best place to hide these crooks. Henry had a policy of hiding someone for no more than three or four days, and then the person would have to leave.

Henry's success in hiding criminals encouraged other farm neighbors to join in the easy money-making opportunity. At any given time, at least two to three farms would serve as a refuge spot for a running criminal. These desperate men would never see the day on a most wanted list, and in time, most would be caught and sent to prison. Before long, Southtown began to develop a reputation as a good place for hiding. This reputation would last over 40 years.

This activity was not overlooked by Tommy or Madge. Both would occasionally hide a small-time crook for a couple of days for as much as $10 to $20 a day. The worse the crime the more their hiding days would cost them. Madge, although not as physically imposing as her younger brother, had a look and demeanor that clearly stated she was not a person to cross. Having a brother with a reputation for beating even the meanest of local characters senseless with his blackjack was more than enough incentive for any crook hiding with Madge and Tommy to behave himself. Their first home had a small half-basement and could hold up to three people. The experience of hiding someone underneath their home would later serve as the prototype for later properties and basement hiding.

TOMMY SCOPES OUT SOUTHEAST KANSAS AND BEGINS HIS LIQUOR RUNS

As soon as Tommy earned enough money as a bouncer, he bought a small motorcycle and used it to travel through town and Coffeyville. He used this new and versatile vehicle to scope out the illegal activity around Coffeyville and to determine the effectiveness of the city's police department. He also used the motorcycle to check out the possible escape routes around Coffeyville and Southtown in the event a Kansas or Oklahoma posse or liquor raid took place. Most of the Coffeyville bars were known to Tommy, and when he was on his motorcycle, they were probably being scoped out. Tommy, the consummate learner, was always on the watch to see what was going on and what he could learn. He quickly realized from his trips to Coffeyville that Southtown's larger northern neighbor was a sin city itself, and Kansas prohibition and gambling laws were so restrictive that the locals were itching to find a better place to party; this situation gave Southtown a lot of room to grow in the world of illegal vices.

Another benefit of his early motorcycle days was the ability to drive just about every vehicle available in the Coffeyville area. Tommy was a quick learner, and driving trucks was one of his specialties. To test the crude Southeast Kansas roads, Tommy used his motorcycle. By the mid-teens, Tommy knew just about every usable road within a 75 radius of Coffeyville. His unique knowledge began to reap financial benefits. In 1913, Tommy started making liquor runs between Galena and Southtown, and the money was good.

During the early teens, Galena, Kansas, a zinc mining town of 7,000, became a principal conduit of illegal liquor coming out of Joplin. Because of the heavily wooded landscape and numerous back roads between both towns, liquor wagons could easily cross the Kansas/Missouri state line with impunity. Knowing the best roads between Galena and Southtown, Tommy was the natural choice to make the liquor runs.

Between 1913 and 1918, Tommy made numerous runs between Galena and Southtown, bringing back as much as 300 bottles of illegal booze per trip. Tommy and two unknown thugs who worked at the Nut House usually made the runs, and they averaged one every two weeks. On one trip during the summer of 1915, the Nut House gang learned that there was a monthly run going on between Joplin and Tulsa involving two men in two motorcars. The cargo normally consisted of anywhere between 30 to 40 cases of whiskey. They usually took place between the 7th and 10th of each month. A catch like this was too much for Tommy to resist. After three months of watching the liquor run leaving Galena, Tommy and three other cohorts in four vehicles caught their quarry. During the early evening of December 9th, two cars and two men carrying 35 cases of whiskey were found just outside Galena, changing a flat tire. Tommy and his crew quickly sprang on the unsuspecting transporters and made them stand by a fence across the road and watch while their whiskey was loaded into the four vehicles. Before departing, Tommy smashed the car's spark plugs to prevent any kind of pursuit. Then, the Nut House crew sped westward to make the transporters think they were heading to somewhere in Kansas. The crew arrived in Coffeyville later that evening, blowing their truck horns to announce that a fresh shipment of booze was heading to Southtown. Coffeyville citizens who heard the blaring horns knew the signal that it was time to head south for a drink. By Midnight, the Southtown bars were serving fresh whiskey.

Thirty-five cases might sound like a lot of booze, but in Southtown, a cache like that might last two weeks. Wanting to make another score without having to pay, Tommy contacted his Galena contacts to determine when another Tulsa run might occur. Unfortunately, the Tulsa-run transporters had elected to mix their run dates and routes to avoid another embarrassing encounter with Tommy and his crew. Nevertheless, Tommy continued to make Galena runs until late 1919, when the Spanish Flu had hit Southeast Kansas so badly that he had to drastically cut his liquor runs and rely more on local stills to keep Southtown somewhat wet. Because of the epidemic, Tommy and Madge decided to stay close to Southtown and hopefully avoid this flu. By being careful and limiting their travel, both were successful in avoiding the epidemic. By mid-1921, the epidemic had subsided, and Tommy was ready to start making some serious money. By this time, Tommy was in his mid-20s and already commanding respect from both locals and patrons. He had a Delaware native make him a special blackjack with a leather strap to wrap his hands around and a leather tip full of steel pellets. One hit from this weapon could knock a person out or break a hand. Tommy was so effective with his blackjack that he seldom carried a pistol. He didn't need to.

With the Volstead Act and nationwide prohibition on liquor then in effect, Tommy decided to turn the liquor runs over to his younger brother Sammy and cousin Fred and concentrate on a new criminal endeavor: bank robbing.

CHAPTER 4
THE BANK ROBBERY, BOOZE AND GANGSTERS ERA

Before delving into the notorious bank robbing and gangster era in the US, particularly after World War I and the Spanish Flu pandemic, it is important to know a little history of how robbing banks evolved in the last half of the 19th Century. Between 1892, the Dalton Raid and the end of World War One (considered by many historians as the modern era of US history), many changes took place. In the following chapters, we will examine those changes and how they affected American crime and bank robbing.

Throughout the second half of the 19th Century, robbing trains, stagecoaches and banks was considered a quick way to make money, providing victims had cash or gold on hand. Gangs were formed, usually consisting of family members and outsiders with reputations for being ruthless. The most famous gangs were the Hole in the Wall gang, the James brothers, and their relatives, the Youngers and Daltons. Throughout this period, which reached a peak in the 1890s, the prey of choice was a small town or local bank. These banks usually held the money of most of the local citizens and could reach a hefty amount (for that era) of $2,000 or more. The money would be a mixture of printed money, gold and silver coins and bank bonds that could be redeemed for cash. The robbers usually struck in daylight and tried to pick times when the downtown area had a sparse crowd. The robbers would move quickly and leave by horseback, hopefully before the locals would have time to respond.

Although most small bank robberies of the era were successful, the cache of stolen money was not always large. Some banks simply did not have very much money in their safes. The first major bank robbery failure was the James gang's attempt to rob the First National Bank in Northfield, Minnesota, in 1876. While the bank robbery was being delayed by a teller who lied about the clock that opened the safe, local citizens noticed that there were two men guarding the front door to the bank. A shootout ensued, leaving all the robbers, except for the James brothers, shot and either wounded or dead. Frank and Jesse James luckily escaped, but they were hounded by a posse for the rest of their lives.

The next big robbery attempt was by the Dalton Gang. The three Dalton brothers and two other robbers attempted to rob two banks at once. The robbery failed, leaving four Coffeyville citizens and four robbers dead.

After the Dalton raid and its deadly failure, bank robberies continued but on a smaller, less frequent scale. But train robberies didn't end. The day after the Coffeyville robbery, the remaining members of the gang robbed a train west of Caney, Kansas. The take wasn't large, but it was enough to motivate the robbers to hide, although they were later caught.

By the turn of the century, life in rural mid-America was changing, and Southeast Kansas, with the largest regional population in the state, changed with the times. When Southtown was incorporated in 1909, Coffeyville and even Nowata had paved streets and sidewalks, electricity, gas, heat, water and sewage services. With the introduction of the Ford Model T in 1905, car ownership grew rapidly, and that growth included law enforcement. Motorcycles, another early transportation marvel, also saw rapid growth.

Another sign of the early 20th-century growth was with banking institutions. The larger banks installed built-in safes that could not be easily opened. Early alarm systems, usually a large sounding bell that could be activated by the push of a button, were also becoming part of a bank's infrastructure. Some alarms had a direct link to the local police station.

Weapon technology also improved, making handguns, rifles and shotguns more deadly. Double-action revolvers became standard by 1900, and the Springfield 1911 semi-automatic pistol soon followed along with other early semi-automatics. Pump action rifles and shotguns, with their reloading speed and improved accuracy, became the norm. Ammunition became smaller but also more deadly. As a result, robbing banks became more difficult, and attempted robberies usually resulting the robbers being killed or quickly caught. In time, robbers would use the new technologies, including the latter use of the Thompson sub-machine gun, better known as the Tommy gun. Cars built for speed and durability also rapidly became the transportation mode of choice, allowing robbers a much better opportunity to reach the border of a neighboring state and avoid being pursued by lawmen. Until J Edger Hoover persuaded Congress in 1933 to pass legislation allowing federal officers to cross state lines and pursue criminals, state, county, and local lawmen had to stop at their jurisdiction borders and allow the criminals they were pursuing to escape. Even though federal marshals and their authority to pursue criminals across the entire country had been around since the mid-19th Century, they were too few and far between. Successful criminals, like the Hole in the Wall gang, had the perfect hideout in Wyoming. They would cross from one state to the next, rob either a train or bank and then flee back to their perfect hideout. It took private Pinkerton agents and an expert tracker to flush this gang out and destroy their network of crime. In the meantime, in rural Kansas, Missouri, Arkansas, and Oklahoma, it was open season for local and regional criminals who knew the growing network of roads they could use for escape, thus avoiding any meaningful pursuit. Even if a posse could be formed, it would have to stop at either county or state lines. Possess that ignored their "boundaries" would usually be stopped by opposing law enforcement officers and forced to return home. Home turf and legal boundaries were closely guarded and protected. Even to this day, authority boundaries among the plethora of legal institutions are still highly coveted.

Since the beginning of banking, particularly in the 19th and early 20th Century, banks have always been considered easy prey for criminals. Surprisingly however, bank robbing was never a fine art. Usually, the robber or group of robbers would try to enter inconspicuously, hold up the teller(s) and make the bank president open the main safe. Like with the Daltons, the local townspeople walking by would usually see that something was wrong and yell for help. In a matter of minutes, the robbers might find themselves surrounded and out of luck. More enterprising robbers would use dynamite or, worse, nitroglycerin to blow the safe open. Some robbers would try this method in daylight, but most preferred blowing safes after dark. For their part, banks would normally rely on hidden guns or the alertness of the locals. Improved criminal technology and better methods of protection would be needed by bank officials and employees. The larger banks embarked on new safety methods, but the same could not be said for the small local banks.

If there was one major flaw in the Kansas banking system, it was the lack of consistent safety procedures in smaller banks. In small Kansas and Oklahoma towns during the early 20th century, there was a lack of modern technology and law enforcement. A small town might be lucky if it could afford a constable, and usually, that person was someone completely lacking in law enforcement training. He was also someone who would probably go to great lengths to avoid being shot. Telephone service was just starting to reach small towns, and usually, it was a crude setup with a local women's operator making the phone connections between listening to conversations to keeping up with local gossip. Making a call to the county sheriff during a robbery was time-consuming and often ended with a failed connection. By the time the sheriff arrived, the robbers were in another county or farther.

Another early problem was with the banks themselves. Because of their rural location, most bankers didn't feel the need for alarms or other preventive measures. For them, keeping a handgun and/or a rifle was enough of a deterrent. They also used small vaults, usually on wheels, and placed them behind the main window of the bank. To the bankers, this display was their way of showing local patrons that the bank's money was safe.

TOMMY INITIATES HIS PLANS TO ROB SMALL BANKS

Tommy, always looking for a better way to make money, noticed on his numerous liquor runs throughout Southeast

Kansas that the banks located in towns of less than 1,000 people were small and particularly vulnerable. His sister Madge was also keeping tabs on recent bank robberies through Southtown contacts and the Coffeyville Journal daily newspaper. Both quickly concluded that robbing a bank in daylight and attempting to force employees to open their safes was time-consuming and normally allowed the local citizens enough time to react and either capture or kill the bandits. The Daltons had paid with their lives attempting to rob two banks at once, and the robbers who followed them didn't appear to be smart enough to learn from previous mistakes.

Tommy and Madge were in the process of formulating a plan to rob small banks, but World War I and, later, the Spanish flu would hamper their plans. The war was a problem because, by 1918, the nation was in the process of full mobilization to fight the Germans in Europe. Southeast Kansas and Coffeyville were heavily involved in war mobilization. Troops and their horses were stationed at the large National Guard armory on South Walnut. Troops who had the money and opportunity to get a pass would naturally head to Southtown and patronize one of the local bars or brothels. With soldiers residing in Coffeyville, it was a bad time to plan and organize a network for robbing banks.

When the war ended in late 1918, the country was immediately plunged into the Spanish Flue pandemic. People everywhere were sick, and businesses, in general, suffered. Unlike today, with unemployment benefits available, workers in 1919-20 didn't have any means of financial relief when they weren't working. Soup kitchens were formed, but their benefits only scratched the surface. As business and wages declined during the pandemic, so did Southtown's notorious activities. Sick men didn't drink or gamble, nor were they particularly interested in paid sex. Staying healthy and hopefully surviving the pandemic was the order of the day. So, once again, Tommy and Madge had to put their plans on hold.

NATIONWIDE PROHIBITION BEGINS

By the end of 1921, the Spanish Flu was essentially over, allowing businesses and companies the opportunity to staff their enterprises fully. Once again, money started flowing in Southtown. Although Kansas and Oklahoma were already dry states, prohibition became a nationwide phenomenon with the passage of the 18th Amendment to the US Constitution.

Although liquor production and sales had been temporarily suspended during World War I with the passage of the Volstead Act, it was the nationwide push to ban all liquor after the war that brought about the 18th Amendment. Ratified by all but two states, the 18th Amendment became the law of the land on January 16, 1919, with enforcement beginning exactly one year later. Since Oklahoma and Kansas were already considered dry states, prohibition was a moot issue. However, with Missouri now part of the nationwide liquor banned, those who wanted to acquire booze and beer would have to be more creative. Even though booze and beer production still existed in Kansas and Oklahoma, they would not be enough. Missouri, with its reliance on beer production as a means of economic stability and employment in Kansas City and St. Louis, resisted. Even though the major beer manufacturers, like Anheuser Bush and others, had to cease production, smaller, secretive manufacturers appeared in both cities and throughout the state. Missouri might have voted to ratify the 18th Amendment, but the state, in general, did not comply. Illegal stills popped up everywhere, particularly in the hills of the Ozarks. Springfield became a major distributor of bootleg liquor produced locally and brought in from major cities. Kansas City was one of the largest violators of federal prohibition laws, with Boss Tom Prendergast and his political machine paying off state and federal regulators to stay away from his various liquor-related enterprises. Before Prohibition began, Prendergast was the major beer and liquor distributor in Kansas City and the surrounding region. He kept bootleg liquor and beer flowing not only to Kansas City but also to eastern Kansas and southern Missouri. Once the bootleg liquor reached the Ozark region, Springfield, being a regional business, railroad hub and manufacturing center, became a point of sale and distribution. Joplin, with its proximity to southeast Kansas, northeast Oklahoma and northern Arkansas, was the perfect conduit to move bootleg liquor and beer into those regions.

TOMMY ESTABLISHES HIMSELF IN SOUTHTOWN

By the time Prohibition became law, Tommy and Madge were perfectly poised to be part of the distribution network from Joplin. They could not only supply Southtown but also utilize the illegal booze network in Coffeyville. By the early 20s, Tommy had developed considerable experience with moving bootleg liquor from Joplin and other parts of Missouri and Oklahoma. He knew how to move products through the four-state region (southeast Kansas, southwest Missouri, northeast Oklahoma and northwest Arkansas). Tommy had also learned that it was better to be the boss and not one of the soldiers. Along with Tommy's expertise in distribution,

Madge had learned how to manage his finances without detection from state and federal authorities.

Starting around 1921 Tommy, along with his distribution enterprise, had developed an interest in opening his own bars and entertainment centers. His first enterprise was surprisingly in Kansas, just south of Coffeyville's city limits.

In the early 20's the main route out of Coffeyville was South Willow Street. Willow would proceed south to the city limits (about a block west of the Natatorium) and then turn into a dirt road with a metal bridge crossing Onion Creek. On the north side of this creek and bridge was a small area that was considered part of Montgomery County. It was the perfect site for a bar. It would be part of the north/south road between Southtown and Coffeyville and was surrounded by a heavily wooded area. To enforce Prohibition laws, the Montgomery County Sheriff's office would either have to drive through Coffeyville or cross into Nowata County, Oklahoma, to reach Tommy's new bar from the south. In the early twenties and to a large degree this day, the legal turf of states, counties and municipalities are still closely guarded. Crossing state lines was particularly forbidden.

With this law enforcement peculiarity in mind, Tommy moved forward and opened his first bar in a small building west of the South Willow Road and north of the Onion Creek Bridge. It would be called the Casa Del Sol. From the beginning, the Casa Del Sol was very popular and not bothered by local law enforcement agencies. However, Tommy's first bar did not last long. Due to pressure from federal prohibition agents, local police and the sheriff's office came to a turf agreement and raided the bar. At first, Tommy attempted to bribe local officials, but with pressure from the federal government to enforce liquor laws, the bribes were ignored, and within a year, the bar was closed. Not wanting another episode of what he experienced with his first bar, Tommy decided it was time to move his entertainment business to Southtown and to work in Oklahoma.

Thus, he moved to Oklahoma and made it his home base. His new venture was a bar and dance hall located just south of the Kansas border and east of the main road through town. It would initially be called Tommie's Roadhouse but would later be changed to the Casa Del Camino. It had an open bar upstairs and a dance floor. But more important, Tommy had a basement dug out to accommodate a room for gambling and another smaller one for hiding a small number of crooks needing a quick place to hide. Its location was hidden by a mirror the size of a door that would electronically pivot open by the push of a strategically placed button. Tommy, along with his sister Madge, had a business that would last almost 40 years.

Even though Tommy kept a residence in Coffeyville to use when he needed to be out of Oklahoma or simply wanted to be close to what was happening in his larger northern neighbor, Tommy's home base would remain Southtown for the rest of his life. Madge would also make Southtown home for the remainder of her long life. Tommy purchased a home west of Southtown just south of the Kansas /Oklahoma road. He always wanted to be close to Kansas in the event a quick exit to the state line was needed. Tommy's first home was unique. Like the Casa Del, Tommy had a basement dug with a special room that could hide up to five individuals behind a revolving mirror that could be electronically opened by pushing a hidden button.

Tommy was fortunate with his timing. He was now living and working in a state with very little effective law enforcement. Oklahoma did not have a state law enforcement agency and wouldn't until the late 20's. Nowata County had a Sheriff's office, but it was underfunded. Its deputies were consistently more concerned with cattle rustling than enforcing Prohibition laws. When the Nowata Sheriff's office became involved, it was usually at the insistence of federal anti-liquor agents. Even though federal liquor agents were located in Oklahoma, mainly Oklahoma City, they were more concerned with keeping illegal liquor away from the various indigenous tribes across the state than troubling themselves with a small town located just south of the northern state line. It was a perfect storm for Tommy and Madge until 1924.

However, on January 9, 1924, federal and Kansas anti-liquor agents from Coffeyville raided Tommie's Roadhouse and found 12 gallons of corn liquor. Tommy and his sister's fiancée, Wick Karns, were arrested. Both would spend time in the Montgomery County Jail in Kansas.

Sensing they had found the source of illegal beer and liquor in the area, federal, Oklahoma and Kansas agents raided Southtown again on August 20, 1924. This time, they raided three locations. The first was the gas station just south of the state line; there, they found nothing. The next location was Bill Hicks's home adjacent to the gas station. There, the agents found a significant cache of illegal liquor and beer. The third location was Tommy's home, a short distance west of town just south of the state line. Tommy, who was still serving a sentence in the Montgomery County Jail, was not present, but his wife was caught emptying a bottle of liquor down the stool of an upstairs bathroom. She successfully emptied the bottle before the agents could catch her. The cache of illegal liquor was large enough to press charges on the Hicks. In their home, 25 gallons of corn liquor and 50 gallons of choc beer were confiscated.

With these two raids, Southtown was now identified and branded at the state and federal level as a place of ill-repute and a haven for the sale and distribution of illegal liquor and beer.

By 1925, Tommy and Wick were out of jail. Wick married Madge and both left on an extended honeymoon. Tommy, ever busy, expanded his local empire. The Casa Del, with its basement for gambling and hiding, was going strong. He built a little shack next to the roadhouse and used it to sell packaged liquor and beer. On the weekends, long lines of customers would form in front of this shed, wanting a bottle of bootleg liquor or beer to take home.

Tommy's Roadhouse was an immediate success. His bar not only served adults but also teenagers who had the money to purchase a drink. Tommy did not enforce age limits but instructed his bouncers to throw anyone out who was clearly too young to be there. That rule was strictly enforced regarding young teenage girls. The last thing Tommy or Madge needed was a young girl getting drunk and raped at or near his establishment. As for teenage boys, the roadhouse became a rite of passage before they became adults. Teen boys had several ways to get to Southtown. If their parents had a car, then it was easy to get the keys with or without parental permission. If that didn't work, then there was the interurban, normally the transportation of choice. It was cheap and ran directly to Southtown drinking establishments. If a teen got too drunk or stayed too late to catch the last trolley, he could simply walk. Coffeyville's main residential area was roughly a mile from Southtown and an easy walk down South Willow. According to Harold Haddan, Newt's son and a rowdy teenager in the 1930s, the South Willow Road was the route of choice for teenage boys too drunk to drive or catch the last Interurban trolley. South Walnut leading south to the new Onion Creek bridge was normally watched by Coffeyville police, and even back in the 20s and 30s, an underage teen did not want his parents to know that he had trekked to Southtown to drink. Even though teen boys were the main source of drinkers under 18, adventurous girls at or close to 18 also made their way south. After all, it was the roaring 20s, a time of prosperity and fun for young people. In 1918, women still wore their dresses at their ankles. By 1925, girls and young women wore their dresses above the knee and forsook the tight girdles their mothers once wore. Sex, dancing, alcohol and "fast" cars were the norm of this period. Coffeyville was no exception to these new norms, and Southtown was the perfect place to exercise this new freedom. Places like Tommie's Roadhouse, the Tavern, and the Nut House were destination places for people, young and old, who wanted a good time. Even prostitution continued to be available, but further south from Tommy's establishment. What Tommie wanted at his establishment was revenue from bootleg liquor, dancing, gambling in the basement and taking money from drunk suckers. As time passed, Tommie's Roadhouse would become the template for other establishments in Southtown.

As the 20s progressed, many changes took place in Southtown. In the small downtown area, a city hall, post office, grocery store and general goods store appeared. In the same vicinity was a drug store owned by Tommy that certainly did more than sell prescription drugs. It also sold bootleg liquor and had a small gambling room in the rear of the store.

Directly across from the post office, a theater was built to house vaudeville acts, music events and movies. It had a large stage for live entertainment and could seat over 500 patrons. A two-story building was built just south of the state line and housed a gas station for early north/south automobile travelers. It also had another sinister reason for existence. The upstairs was used for poker games, and there was an attached shed where bootleg liquor was sold. The station also had a tunnel that led across the main road to another establishment called the Southern Club. This building was of brick and stucco and had a full basement with an indoor and outdoor entrance. The upstairs was used primarily for drinking and dancing. The downstairs had a full bar and tables for poker and craps. Of course, the "house" would ultimately win, giving the owners plenty of illegal revenue. And who were the owners? Wick Karns and Tommy's younger brother, Claude "Sandy" Hill and Madge.

Around 1924, Madge met Wick Karns, fell in love and married him a year later. Wick was a local man of means. He owned land and made a small fortune drilling gas and oil. Upon meeting and courting Madge, he quickly learned the extent of her enterprises and elected to join but as a more silent partner. After their marriage, Wick and Madge purchased a home in Southtown and started the process of forming a family business involving his wife, Tommy, and

Sandy. Tommy would be the front man, with Wick, Madge and Sandy handling the real estate and money behind the scenes. Wick and Sandy also handled the purchase and distribution of bootleg liquor to the various bars in Southtown and the gas station.

Wick purchased a ranch close to the Noxie, Oklahoma, rail ramp and placed it in Sammy's name. Sammy and Tommy would use the ranch to hide criminals for a fee. The more notorious the criminal, the higher the fee. The ranch would be named Timber Hill.

Sandy Hill, nine years younger than Tommy, was only 20 when he joined the family enterprise. Sandy was smart and quickly learned about the family business. Wick was an expert gambler and taught Sandy how to cheat without being caught. He also taught Sandy how to keep a low profile. From this point until his death in 1953, Sandy, as well as Wick, would never be prosecuted for more than selling illegal liquor. Madge was also an expert at keeping a low, respectful profile. In later years, she would be known as a person of means and willingness to help those in dire need. The same could not be said for Tommy. He was always testing the legal limits of his crimes.

THE ROARING 20S IS IN FULL SWING IN SOUTHTOWN

By the mid-20s, Southtown was coming into its own as a town of ill-repute, with more bars opening; these additions only added to the town's seedy reputation. The Nut House had moved closer to the center of town and reduced its size to a small sleazy bar known more for the fighting between patrons than its liquor. Another prominent establishment called the Tavern, sprang up just south of the state line. It was a series of connecting buildings. According to George Elliot, a long-time Southtown resident, the Tavern's first building was a bar for regular patrons and travelers. Through the rear were two additional attached buildings that housed the gambling operation. Poker tables, roulette, and craps were the games of choice at the Tavern. Poor losers at the tables or just general drunken behavior were enough to get someone bounced out of the Tavern and thrown over to the Kansas side of the state line. According to Elliot, Harry Houdini, the famous magician who performed at the Jefferson Theater in Coffeyville, visited the Tavern after a performance and was shot over an argument. The wound was obviously superficial. Biographies on Houdini do not mention the incident, however.

Another club that would gain notoriety over the next 10 years was the Southern Club, located close to the post office.

At this point, there is some controversy over the exact name of Tommy's bar by the gas station. The 1928 federal court case refers to it as Tommie Hill's Roadhouse. Other accounts indicate that at the time Madge was indicted in federal court in 1928, Tommy had already changed the name to the Casa Del Camino. In time, the roadhouse would be referred to as simply the Casa Del. It would become a popular place to drink and dance for the next 30 years.

THE FEDS MAKE THEIR FIRST ATTEMPT TO SHUTDOWN SOUTHTOWN

In 1926, Madge Karns was issued a federal notice to cease and desist from serving illegal liquor in the roadhouse the feds alleged she owned. In reality, Wick was probably co-owner with Madge, but she took the rap. Madge refused to comply and was indicted on federal charges. During the court proceedings, which didn't end until late 1928, the judge found her in Contempt of Court. She was convicted, fined $500 and sentenced to six months in jail. Even though there had been an earlier injunction to cease selling bootleg liquor, Madge, along with Wick and Tommy, again refused to comply. All were found in contempt of court, but Madge took the brunt of the bad publicity. For his part, Federal District Judge Franklin Kennamer went a step further and had most of the major alleged drinking establishments closed and padlocked for 12 months. Even the recently raided drug store owned by Tommy was shut down. Despite pleas to keep it open for medical reasons, Judge Kennamer refused to lift his ban on the place. With Southtown temporarily closed, it was time for Tommy to expand his bank-robbing exploits and hide criminals, preferably with high profiles. Hiding them would earn Tommy considerably more money. All he needed was a quick way to transport them from major cities to Southtown and avoid being caught.

By the late 20s aviation had matured, from rickety biplanes to more sophisticated aircraft. First, Tommy learned to fly. Then he purchased a Cessna Model A, a single-engine,four-seater airplane and some land where the South Coffeyville Stockyards is currently located and built a hanger. Across from the hanger, Tommy purchased additional land south for a landing strip. The Cessna served Tommy well for about six months, but when two of his employees tried to fly the aircraft and crashed it, Tommy had to find another plane. During a quick search at Tulsa's new municipal airport, he found a Douglas C1 single-engine four-seat plane. It was an excellent aircraft and served Tommy well.

After the 12-month bar closure injunction ended, bars could open again. One of Tommy's first acts as a pilot was to fly over Coffeyville, blowing a horn to announce he had a fresh load of bootleg liquor for sale. He would slowly circle the town using a special horn attached to the outside of the plane that could be blown with a special electric button on his control panel. The horn was so loud that one blast could be heard halfway across Coffeyville. Tommy's flying escapes did not stop there. During his earlier liquor run days to Joplin, Tommy had developed contacts with the criminal element there. Joplin was developing into a criminal conduit from Kansas City to Hot Springs, Arkansas, giving criminals a safe passage and occasional stopover between both cities.

Hot Springs, designated in 1921 as a national park and a town lined with bathhouses, was a favorite place for politicians, celebrities, and mobsters. In 1926, Mayor Leo McCauliffe became mayor and made gambling legal at the local level. Mobsters like Lucky Luciano, Al Capone, and Owney Madden became frequent visitors. Madden liked the town so much that he permanently settled there, sending the signal that Hot Springs was the place for criminals to stay and avoid arrest. Federal agents tried to infiltrate and arrest any criminal staying at Hot Springs, but local interference usually frustrated their efforts.

Despite the availability of Hot Springs as a "safe haven," the cost to get them through Joplin or Tulsa was expensive and dangerous. With federal agents constantly looking for criminals on roads and railroad lines that led to Hot Springs, a person on the run from the law was constantly looking over his shoulder. For criminals who feared they would not be able to complete the trip, they chose to pay Tommy to fly them to Southtown to hide until they could complete their journey.

With his contacts in Joplin, Tulsa, and from some of the more prominent criminals he hid, Tommy was able to establish a connection to the criminal element in Chicago. During the 20s, Chicago was run by the Capone and O'Banion mobs. It was the time of the "roaring 20s," and Chicago was right in the middle of it. With the Volstead Act in place, illegal booze and beer flowed through Chicago. With the large amount of money that could be made selling illegal liquor, the various Chicago gangs were constantly at war with each other, looking for an advantage in the liquor market. Gang killings were almost a daily occurrence. With each gang killing, the hit men involved were constantly looking for a place to hide.

Even though interstate pursuit was still years away, the treasury department already had an internal most wanted list and regularly contacted state and local law enforcement agencies for assistance. Traveling for someone on the run from the law could be hazardous, but Tommy had a perfect solution. He would fly to Chicago and secretly pick up the criminal needing to hide and fly him to Southtown.

By the mid-20s, Tommy developed three places to hide criminals. For very short stays, a criminal could hide in the little basement room behind the revolving mirrored door at the Casa Del. For longer stays, maybe a few days, Tommy would hide them in his new hanger. For extended stays and more money, the Timber Hill Ranch, west of Southtown, would be available. In the middle 20s the ranch was in a heavily wooded area of Nowata County. It was located five miles away from Southtown, and the only road to the ranch was little more than a rough path. The ranch itself contained a small house and two outbuildings. By the late 20's and early 30's, Southtown would be considered a safe place for criminals to hide. The bigger the criminal, the more money Tommy could charge.

Tommy couldn't replicate Hot Springs and its lavish hotels, but he could offer the kind of low-profile safety many criminals liked. He also charged less. As a result, Southtown became a destination point for criminals needing to hide until the "heat" was off. Two early criminals who gave Southtown their seal of approval as a hiding place were Pretty Boy Floyd and Alvin Karpis. Others, like Frank Nash, Al Richetti, Harry Campbell, and Glenn Roy Wright, would also enjoy Southtown's hospitality as a hiding place. They found the Casa Del to be the best place in town. There was plenty of liquor, a large dance floor, pretty girls to dance with, and a poker game in the basement. If state or federal authorities decided to pay a visit, there was the hidden room behind the mirrored door.

At one point, Southtown became very close to being exposed. On January 15, 1932, due to the number of bank robberies in Oklahoma and Pretty Boy Floyd's criminal notoriety, Acting Governor Robert Burns and the Adjutant General of the Oklahoma National Guard, Charles Barrett, held a special meeting in Oklahoma City with the Sheriffs of five counties on how they could work together to stop Floyd and other bank robbers. The Nowata County Sheriff was not invited. The National Guard would not commit troops but offered equipment when needed. After the meeting, state law enforcement officers joined the deputies from the five counties to scour northeast Oklahoma for Floyd and his gang, plus any other bank robbers they could find. Area federal marshals also joined in the search. This intense search went on for over three months but turned up little more than a handful of minor criminals. Floyd and his gang escaped thanks to the help offered by Tommy and Wick. This would not be the last time Floyd would ask for help. After the June 1933 Union Station Massacre in Kansas City, Floyd and his partner, Al Richetti, would again ask for assistance. Because of the intense heat being brought to bear by the newly armed Federal Bureau of Investigation (FBI), Floyd and Richetti's stay would be short. They hid at the Timber Hill Ranch for several days and left Oklahoma for good.

RACIAL TENSIONS IN SOUTHEAST KANSAS

Even though Southtown's illegal activities appeared to be on the rise, other issues were simmering below the surface. Ever since the Supreme Court ruled against Blacks with the Plessy vs. Ferguson decision, America had slowly but fervently slid into an era of racial segregation. Blacks were forced to live like third-class citizens. In the Southeast, their lives were not different. Kansas, for its part, sent a confusing message. During the Civil War and afterward, eastern Kansas was considered a haven for former Black slaves. Many communities had significant Black minorities. Coffeyville had the largest in Southeast Kansas. Despite the influx of Blacks, Kansas Whites ensured that this minority would not receive any preferential treatment during segregation. In fact, Topeka, the state's capitol, would be the subject of denying a Black girl access to a white school and its music program. That denial eventually led to the Supreme Court decision in the early 1950s that would end segregation in America forever.

However, in the 1920s, Coffeyville was segregated with clear racial boundaries.

Oklahoma was as bad or worse. In a fairly new state already accustomed to racial discrimination with its indigenous population, Oklahoma also had clear racial segregation boundaries. Blacks living in White majority communities would live in segregated areas and take what menial jobs were available to them. On the other hand, because Oklahoma, a new state lacking the racial history of other states, allowed Blacks to form their own communities. During the 1920s, there were 13 all-Black communities in Oklahoma. Boley and Langston were and are still today the largest of these small towns. Other communities, like Lenapah, would have a unique racial mix of Whites, Blacks and Native Americans. Although a small town with a railroad and regional interurban trolley line, Lenapah had a robust economy and a surprisingly large number of Blacks living in and around the community. They were a very closely knitted group of families and mostly worked in Coffeyville and Southtown when jobs for Blacks were available. Southtown, which had only one or two Black families living outside the city limits, did not readily accept Blacks with open arms. The people of Southtown in the 1920s and later were a tough bunch who were suspicious of new people moving to the town. Blacks were especially discouraged. According to a former Southtown resident, Lonnie Lee, who grew up in a tough environment, had to learn early how to defend himself. In later years, he would gain some notoriety as a bare-knuckle boxer. During his formative years, Lonnie ran with the Southtown boys, and they were a bunch to be avoided. Teens from Coffeyville would occasionally travel south to prove how tough they were. On just about every occasion, the Coffeyville boys were sent packing home with black eyes and other physical "souvenirs." Blacks, for their part, knew better and stayed north of the state line. Going to Southtown to replenish Coffeyville's Black community's supply of liquor and beer was their primary experience south of the state line.

With this background on Oklahoma race relations in mind, there was one community with a unique racial situation. Tulsa, a city with over 100,000 and tremendous oil and gas wealth by 1920, had a segregated area called the Greenwood district. It was a well-organized sub-community that learned the benefits of circulating its money primarily within. As a result, Greenwood became a prosperous part of Tulsa with its own banks, theatre, doctors, lawyers, and shopping area. It was called the "Black Wall Street" of the US and was a one-of-a-kind success story.

In 1921, a mistaken racial encounter between a White girl and a Black boy in an elevator would lead to the worst race riot and massacre in US history. By the time the riot was over, the entire Greenwood district would be destroyed by fire, and close to 300 Blacks were dead. It would take the Greenwood district almost eight years to rebuild but even then, not entirely.

Tulsa wasn't the only community close to Southtown to experience racial violence. On a cold December 17, 1921 evening, Independence, Kansas, an affluent community 18 miles north of Southtown, experienced a racial riot. On that date, a Black man allegedly shot and killed a White grocer;

the Black man was arrested and held in the Montgomery County Courthouse jail. Local Blacks, armed with rifles and pistols, approached the courthouse. Local Whites met them, and shots were fired, resulting in the deaths of Black and White citizens. The situation became so tense that local Kansas National Guard troops were mobilized to stop the violence. Luckily, there wasn't any property damage, but before the violence ended, six more local citizens were wounded by gunfire.

Six years later, Coffeyville almost suffered the same fate as Tulsa and Independence. According to the New York Times publication, on March 17, 1927, two White girls living in a White neighborhood ran out of their house at 1:30 am claiming that they had been raped by three Black men. Three Blacks were arrested, and when the girls had trouble identifying them, they were released. A private investigator hired by the Coffeyville City Council stated that he believed rapists to be Whites in blackface. Two of the three Blacks were escorted home, but by this time, word was circulating through Coffeyville and within a short time, between 1,500 and 3,000 Whites were congregating around City Hall. Like Tulsa, this crowd crossed the railroad tracks and started burning several Black homes. Some of the crowd stayed outside City Hall and started breaking windows, trying to enter. Scared that the Black man still in Custody would be lynched, several police officers hid him on the City Hall roof.

In the meantime, over 100 Blacks and the remaining police officers met the White rioters who had already vandalized several stores, breaking into one to get rifles and ammunition. Shots were fired from both sides, and fortunately, only one White and two Blacks were injured. By this time, the local National Guard arrived and broke up both groups and put up a protection corridor between the White and Black sectors. Independence in 1921 and Coffeyville six years later, had avoided another Tulsa incident, but these unfortunate encounters would leave scars of racial hate and mistrust between Coffeyville and Independence Whites and Blacks that have remained for almost 100 years.

As for Southtown, the race incident north of the state line did not spread south. However, race relations for both communities remained harshly segregated. Not wanting to offend its White customers, Southtown would make a point to ensure that Blacks were not welcome there. In both Coffeyville and Southtown, there was a saying that a Black better not be caught in Southtown after dark if he valued his life. Southtown was a town that served Whites only, but that unofficial rule didn't stop the flow of bootleg liquor reaching the Coffeyville Black community from Oklahoma.

CHAPTER 5
TOMMY'S BANK ROBBING DAYS

During the spring of 1923, Tommy met a farmer from the Mannford, Oklahoma area. His name was Ira Brackett, and he had a unique idea of robbing banks. During his early "rum running" days through Southeast Kansas, Tommy had noticed that the banks in small towns used mobile safes with wheels. These safes were small and round. They also were normally placed behind the main front window of the bank to show the local patrons that their money was safe. Tommy wondered about the vulnerability of these small, local banks but had other priorities with the expanding liquor business in Southtown. Brackett, on the other hand, noticed the same vulnerability and had developed a plan for Tommy to ponder. Instead of breaking into a bank and attempting to open the safe, why not remove it and do the opening at a remote location? To accomplish this kind of theft, Brackett envisioned using a heavy-duty truck with a large motor and flatbed. On the bed, he would install a heavy winch that would lift the safe out of the bank and take it to a remote field to be opened. Tommy liked the idea and decided to join forces with Brackett.

To start the project, Tommy financed the truck, with Bracket doing the purchase and modifications. Brackett would also be responsible for hiring his gang and selecting the banks. Because of the current rash of bank robberies in Kansas and Oklahoma, state and federal investigators relied on determining a pattern of bank heists to help them catch the robbers. The plan of developing a pattern had been pioneered by famous Texas Ranger, Frank Hamer. Hamer was very good at catching his prey and would later use his formula to catch the famous bank robbers Bonnie and Clyde.

Although not always the case, most bank robbers followed a particular geographical route so they would be in a part of a state familiar to them. Tommy, on the other hand, had a better idea. The robberies he planned occurred all over the state of Kansas and didn't have a particular pattern. To keep law enforcement investigators guessing, an occasional robbery in Oklahoma and Arkansas would occur. Tommy also had another stipulation for these heists. He would not be directly involved in any bank robbery. He would finance any up-front money needed and handle the money after each robbery. Tommy also agreed to provide a hiding place for the robbers if their activities got too "hot." It was a "win-win" situation for all parties involved.

The first robbery took place in Atlanta, Kansas. This bank was very small and perfect for the initial heist. The robbery went off without a hitch. The safe was loaded onto the truck and transported to a remote farm in Northeast Oklahoma and opened. Brackett thought of going to Mannford to open the safe but decided to leave it on the field to be found later. The next heist was Piedmont, Kansas, another small town between Fredonia and Augusta. It was another perfect heist. Again, Brackett decided to leave the safe in the field of a remote farm not too far away and avoid being caught on the way to Mannford. Brackett's plan was working perfectly. He kept his gang small with about three other unknown crooks who he trusted to remain loyal. As the robberies continued,

Brackett would change accomplices to avoid any sudden disloyalty due to greed. For his part, Tommy would take his cut and make sure Brackett would stay loyal to him. During the time of these robberies, Tommy had developed a reputation for being a person to avoid crossing. Disloyalty meant a violent beating or a quick and unpleasant death.

SOUTHTOWN CONTINUES TO FLOURISH AS A CITY OF SIN

During the late 20s and early 30s, Tommy, Madge, Wick and Sandy continued to prosper. The oil boom was still going strong, and this boom made Wick a prosperous man. Sandy was managing the properties the family-owned, and Madge remained behind the scenes managing the money. The Casa Del, as it was called by then, was booming. Despite the deepening of the Great Depression, people in Coffeyville and Southeast Kansas continued to work and spend their money in Southtown. Bootleg liquor continued to be served in the growing number of Southtown bars, and gambling and prostitution were available to those who could afford to play and pay. The Southern Club, Tavern, Silver Slipper, and Hi Ho Club had opened in the 1920s, and all continued to boom despite the effects of the growing depression. The Willow Road from Coffeyville was replaced by a new highway and Onion Creek bridge that ran from South Walnut. The new road was designated U.S. Highway 169 and ran all the way from Overland Park, Kansas, to Tulsa. The new highway, although still only partially paved, especially in Oklahoma, rapidly became a major north/south transportation route. And it ran through Southtown and very close to its bars.

Tommy was always looking for new opportunities, and to keep himself in good standing with state and federal law enforcement agencies, he would occasionally turn a crook in for the reward. As usual for this point in his criminal career, Tommy remained above the law and avoided any thought of arresting him. These ventures made Tommy and his family lots of money, but it was the bank robbing that held his interest.

TOMMY'S BANK ROBBING REACHES ITS ZENITH

Throughout the notorious bank robbing days of the 20s and first half of the 30s, 40 to 50 bank robberies a year were common in Oklahoma. Kansas was almost as bad, averaging 20 bank robberies annually. Without the ability to pursue criminals beyond a state and sometimes county line, law enforcement was hamstrung. They were also very slow to purchase the cars and weapons capable of capturing or killing fleeing bank robbers. Knowing the limitations of his adversary's capabilities, Tommy flourished, at least for the moment. His technique of robbing small rural banks with round portable safes was perfect. Banks in the following towns were robbed either directly or indirectly by Tommy's winch removal system:

- Arma Bank, Arma, KS
- Piedmont Bank, Piedmont, KS
- Perry Bank, Perry, KS
- Picher (OK) Bank
- Leroy State Bank, Leroy, KS
- Bank of Elkins Ark*
- Benton Bank, KS*
- Sheldon State Bank, Sheldon MO*

- Trousdale State Bank, Trousdale, KS*
- Alma State Bank, Alma, AR*
- Goodland State Bank, Goodland, KS*
- Bank of Oxford, KS, Jan. 16, 1933*

The safes from the banks with asterisks were recovered on Brackett's Mannford farm.

It must be noted that there were other banks where the safe was stolen, and the criminals caught claimed to be part of Tommy's gang. One bank safe theft occurred in Hastings, Nebraska, in 1931 and was attributed to Tommy. The geographical spread of these robberies demonstrated that Tommy's alleged bank robberies might have stretched further than law enforcement agencies anticipated at the time.

The Bank of Oxford robbery was Tommy's last. Eleven thousand dollars were stolen from its safe, prompting a major push by the Kansas Highway Patrol to catch the robbers. According to the August 17, 1934, Lawrence Journal-World, Brackett had been suspected of the truck winch robberies, which prompted the Oklahoma Creek County Sheriff's office to assist the Kansas officers with their pursuit. The two agencies found Brackett at his Mannford farm with another member of his gang and captured both. Brackett's winch truck was also found in his barn. After some intense questioning, Brackett revealed the location where seven safes were buried on his farm. Brackett, who was 43 at the time of his arrest, would later be extradited to Kansas and sentenced to 15 years in the Lansing State Prison. He would not implicate his silent partner until years later when Tommy was sentenced to life in the Lansing State Prison for another robbery.

According to the May 30, 1937, issue of the Miami Daily News Record, Brackett attempted to make a deal with the State of Kansas by implicating Tommy in the bank robberies. To sweeten his deal attempt, Brackett took Kansas and Oklahoma authorities to his farm and helped excavate several bank safes buried there. Brackett's deal was not accepted, and he spent his entire term in prison.

With Brackett in prison and the winch truck gone, Tommy's bank-robbing days were over. However, he wasn't ready to quit. If banks were no longer an option, there were other businesses who kept large amounts of money in their offices. Utility companies, with their downtown locations in every town of any size, were particularly vulnerable to theft and, so far, had been left alone. Tommy knew that the Union Gas companies kept large amounts of money to handle customer payments. Coffeyville, with its large population, would be an ideal place to rob when the time was right.

The "O. K.," The First Hotel

1. Early Southtown photo.

Eye on the Past

Undated

This South Coffeyville School class picture is believed taken sometime between 1915 and 1920. Standing seventh form left is Tommy Hill, while sitting third from left is Fremont Stark.

2. High school phto with Tommy Hill standing.

3. Coffeyville South Walnut Whore house on 2nd floor.

4. South Walnut, Coffeyville.

5. Drawomg of the winch truck used by Ira Brackett.

(Courtesy Jason Lee)

6. Coffeyville hotel where Pretty Boy Floyd stayed.

7. Tommy Hill's 1936 mug shot.

Tuesday, June 1, 1937

Law Gets Southwest Gang Chief Who Hid Floyd, Karpis and Nash

8. Ira Brackett with bank safe.

ent Reports Bombing

Law Gets Southwest Gang Chief Who Hid Floyd, Karpis and Nash

Ira Brackett, Mannford, Okla., farmer and bank robber, is shown above, during a furlough, digging up one of the many stolen safes hidden on his farm by Hill's hideout gang.

By NEA Service

SOUTH COFFEYVILLE, Kas., May 2[illegible]—Tommy Hill, the stocky South Coffeyville roadhouse keeper, was proud of his brains. For 20 years they maintained him as the crime overlord who ruled the Southwest's worst gangsters in a fantastic, through-the-looking-glass stronghold. But he is deposed now.

Still in his early forties, Hill is under one sentence of life imprisonment—a Kansas state sentence as an habitual criminal. He also is under a two-year federal term for mail robbery. He had appealed the life sentence and was out on bond when the federal men arrested him as "finger-man" in the Cof-

TOMMY HILL

9. Newspaper clipping of Tommy Hill and Ira Bracket.

10. Southtown gas station and Casa Del looking north.

11. Southtown looking north on US 169.

12. Former Pete and Kelly's bar and café(demolished 2024)

13. Former Southtown bar.

14. Former Southtown barber shop and bar to the right.

15. Casa Del nightclub and dancehall.

16. Club Royal advertisement.

17. Tommy Hill's blackjack (courtesy Ed Todd).

18. Coffeyville Police Chief Pete Billups & Assitant Police Chief Art Gamble-1950.

19. Wick and Madge Karns former residence.

20. Southtown Southern Supper Club with gambling den (closed).

21. Bob Folk's Southtown motel with the Tavern on the right-1957.

22. Bob Folk dancing.

23. Bob Folk at a casino.

24. Bones Cafe.

CHAPTER 6
TOMMY'S DOWNFALL

Tommy's time as the "Crime overlord of Oklahoma" and the "go-to" person for hiding criminals on the run started to unravel in 1933. There were several reasons. First, he involved himself in the Coffeyville Union Gas Office robbery that year. In addition, Tommy was almost caught in a botched attempt to sell stolen bonds in Miami, Oklahoma, and later, he was accused of robbing a mail truck for $4. If that were not enough, Tommy was also accused of being involved in another gas utility office robbery in northeast Kansas. Finally, Kansas state law enforcement agencies, spearheaded by Detective Joe Anderson, were hot on Tommy's trail over the numerous small-town bank robberies he was allegedly involved in.

To deter detection, Tommy would occasionally turn in a criminal he was hiding. The most notable was Ray Terrill, a career criminal who paid Tommy handsomely to fly him to Hot Springs to hide. Tommy flew Terrill to Hot Springs but into the hands of waiting federal agents. He had tipped them off in hopes of raising his status of being a model citizen. It was about this time that Tommy would occasionally brag that he was much smarter than law enforcement agents and would always be one step ahead of them.

Anderson's pursuit of Tommy wasn't the time Southtown had aroused state or federal attention. Federal agents had been snooping around Southtown since the 20s. In 1932, federal agents came to town looking for information on the kidnapping of Charles Lindberg's child. They started at the Kansas/Oklahoma state line and proceeded south, looking throughout the town for the child. The agents were aware of the alleged tunnels and might have found them, except news arrived that the baby had been found dead beside a road near the Lindberg's New Jersey residence. The search was called off and after the agents left, Southtown went back to business as usual.

Four years later, another incident occurred that brought federal agents back to Southtown. According to an FBI document dated December 1936, Agents from Kansas City and Oklahoma City converged on Southtown searching for information regarding the kidnapping of Edward Bremer.

According to Michael Newton's The Encyclopedia of Kidnappings, the kidnapping of Edward Bremer is considered the last major criminal enterprise of the Barker-Karpis gang. Even though the gang was successful in netting a large ransom, the full force of the FBI was brought to bear against it, resulting in the death or capture of its main members several months later. The kidnapping was ordered by St. Paul Jewish-American organized crime boss Harry Sawyer and carried out by Fred Barker, Alvin Karpis, Arthur Barker, Volney Davis and Chicago mobster George Zeigler.

The document made it clear that Southtown was on the FBI's radar and Tommy was a principal character. The document mentioned Sandy, another relative, Fred Hill, and Wick Karns. The person the agents were looking for was Milt Lett, a resident of Wann, Oklahoma and a person of interest regarding Fred Barker and Alvin Karpis. The agents conducted an extensive search and questioned numerous Southtown and Coffeyville residents but could not learn anything about the whereabouts of Lett. Tommy was mentioned in the report, but agents decided to decline to interview him. They determined that Tommy was so upset over his recent conviction as a habitual criminal he was not worth interviewing. One person mentioned in the document was Harry Sherman, better known as "Boogy Woogy." Sherman worked at the Nut House as a bartender and bouncer and considered most people who knew him as a habitual liar. Federal agents decided to drop him from their interview list and soon after left the area.

THE CRIMINALS WHO EVENTUALLY CONTRIBUTED TO TOMMY'S ARREST

In the early to mid-1930s, a new kind of criminal appeared. They were usually men of modest means who came from poor families trying to stay one step ahead of the depression gripping the nation. These men and sometimes their women were probably not educated above the sixth grade and had spent time in juvenile reform schools for petty crimes and belligerent behavior. Men like John Dillinger, Charles, "Pretty Boy" Floyd, Baby Face Nelson, Wilber Underhill, Frank Nash, Alvin Karpis, Ma Barker and her boys and Bonnie and Clyde were the type of criminals who lived for the moment and were not afraid of death. They started their crime spree for either quick cash and/or the thrill of robbing a bank and getting away. It usually didn't take most of them very long to become murderers. These criminals robbed banks, and tellers or guards often pursued them. Their foolish bravery sometimes cost them their lives. Nash, Floyd and Dillinger didn't want to kill anyone but wouldn't tolerate an over-zealous bank employee chasing them with a gun. Once the killing started, it was impossible for the gangsters to reverse the chain of events and the consequences.

Despite their occasional recklessness, these criminals were smart enough to stay ahead of the law. They drove fast cars, used Tompson submachine guns and had Browning Automatic Rifles (BARs). They also wore armored vests when available. These crooks knew their territory, which banks to rob and how to cross state lines without being caught. And they occasionally drove through Southtown for a good time and when needed, a place to hide from law enforcement. Tommy had the Casa Del basement, his airplane hanger and the Timber Hill Ranch. Thanks to visits from these early criminal days, Karpis and Floyd put the word out that Southtown was a haven where criminals could rely on Tommy, along with his family. Floyd, an Oklahoma native and a person who liked to live dangerously, would go a step further and, like his other criminal counterparts, would spend the night at the Alvin Hotel or an apartment above the Sears and Roebuck store in downtown Coffeyville. It was a perfect place for him. The Alvin was a small three-story hotel close to the railroad tracks. By today's standards, it was a very plain and cheap hotel that didn't ask questions. The apartment, believed by many Floyd historians to be the residence of his estranged wife, gave him a chance to see his son. Coffeyville locals also knew Floyd often used the apartment to be a place for his waiting spouse. It was there that Newt Haddan, a friend of Floyd's, caught Floyd going down the alley fire escape one morning and warned him that the Coffeyville police were looking for him. Despite his many overnight stays in Coffeyville, Floyd was never caught there.

Helping criminals like Karpis, Doc Barker, Floyd, Frank Nash and Adam Richette gave Tommy a chance to expand his contacts in other cities, most notably in Chicago and with the Capone mob. Tommy would fly to Chicago or a nearby town, pick up a particular criminal, and fly the person back to Southtown. The notoriety of the criminal would determine where he was hidden and how much he was charged. Depending on the person and the crime(s), Tommy could charge in excess of $1,000. In 1931, $1,000 was a huge sum, and this kind of transaction kept Tommy and his family rolling in cash.

There has been considerable discussion from Coffeyville and Southtown natives concerning the time Bonnie and Clyde allegedly drove through Southtown. Officially, there isn't any solid evidence that the gang was either in Southtown or Coffeyville after the Commerce, Oklahoma murders in 1933. The Coffeyville scene in the Netflix movie "The Highwaymen," depicting the Barrow's stopping in town long enough to get some medicine for Bonnie's leg, did not occur. Newt Haddan, always a great storyteller, never mentioned any episode involving Coffeyville when the 1967 movie "Bonnie and Clyde" came out. In addition, Newt's son, Harold, age 15 at the time of the alleged event, would have known about any downtown event involving the famous gang. He, too, never mentioned them being in town. However, despite the lack of physical evidence or eyewitnesses, stories about Bonnie and Clyde stopping in Southtown for a very short visit continue to be posted on Coffeyville's Facebook historical sites. During the 1980s, three South Coffeyville residents who were old enough to remember 1933 swore they saw Bonnie and Clyde stopping to get gas and going to the Casa Del. In addition, former Southtown resident Mike Reister shared a story about his father working at the Casa Del as a bouncer. Mike's father never mentioned seeing Bonnie and Clyde, but while he was working at the Casa Del, it was common knowledge that they had been there. The only person who claimed later to have served both robbers liquor and some food from the Casa Del's kitchen was a man whose name has been lost to history, but his alleged nickname was the "big bouncer." His story started the Bonnie and Clyde episode in Southtown and has never been refuted. Therefore, it is safe to conclude that the gang stopped in Southtown before leaving for Fort Scott, Kansas.

Even though Tommy was making money selling his bootleg liquor, gambling, and hiding criminals, he considered robbing the Coffeyville Union Gas office. On a cold day on January 5, 1933, five criminals entered the Casa Del looking for Tommy. They were Harry Campbell, Tommy Carpenter, Jimmy Lawson, Clarence Spencer, and Glenn Roy Wright. The group approached Tommy about a quick way to get some cash to finance a job they were planning in Kansas City. Tommy made the first major mistake of his life by agreeing to help them. Tommy had considered robbing the Coffeyville Union Gas office on several occasions but had backed out at the last minute. With the opportunity to involve other men and potentially avoid any potential direct involvement himself, Tommy suggested that heist to the gang. Of course, he demanded a slice of the action, so Tommy agreed to go to the office shortly before they planned to rob it, pay his gas bill and scope it for them.

On January 9, the robbery went off without any violence; the gang took $2,545 in cash. Within a year, all but Harry Campbell and Tommy had been arrested and quickly sentenced to prison. Campbell would avoid arrest for another two years before being caught and prosecuted. By this time, the law was closing in on Tommy.

During his bank robbing days, Tommy accumulated a sizable sum of negotiable bonds. On June 19, 1933, Tommy gave two small-time crooks $21,300 in bonds to sell in Miami, Oklahoma. The transaction went horribly. The crooks, Emmett Jones and Cy Briggs, accidentally tried to sell the bonds to a federal agent posing as a buyer from Tulsa. The transaction was set to occur outside a Miami dance hall north of town. As soon as Jones and Briggs showed the bonds they were selling, four federal agents came from behind several parked cars and quickly apprehended the two men. With a little tough persuasion, they told the agents where Tommy was.

While waiting in the Picher, Oklahoma Connell Hotel, Tommy learned of the disaster and quickly hurried back to Southtown. The federal agents missed him by 10 minutes. Oklahoma and Kansas state law enforcement agencies were immediately notified of the botched bond sale and issued an arrest warrant for Tommy. He was later arrested at the Casa Del by Kansas state detectives who illegally crossed the Oklahoma state line and was sent to the Montgomery County Jail in Independence, Kansas. Since federal authority to supersede state and local jurisdictions hadn't been approved by the US Congress yet, the agents had to drop their arrest warrant and were forced to turn over their evidence to the Montgomery County District Court. He would be tried by the county for the attempted sale of $25,000 in stolen Liberty Loss bonds from a July 19, 1933 mail truck robbery.

The district attorney at the time was a lawyer named Richard Becker from Coffeyville. Becker had a reputation for being a very smart and skilled courtroom attorney. As a district attorney, Becker proved himself to be very resourceful in gathering evidence and witnesses. He also excelled in cross-examining defendants.

When the stolen bond sale attempt came before him, Becker knew that Tommy's days evading the law were coming to an end. In this case, he had stolen bonds from three banks.

The stolen bonds came from three banks:

$5,600 from the Gravette, ARK Bank, September 1932

$5,700 from the Decatur ARK Bank, December 1932

$ 10,000 from a bank in Neosho Falls, KS, December 1932, two nights before.

EVENTS THAT LED TO TOMMY'S CONVICTION

By 1932, Kansas Law Enforcement had also decided to close in on Tommy. They had long suspected that he had been the brains behind numerous bank robberies that used the pickup winch system and hauled the safes off. Tommy was also implicated as part of several robberies of utility companies and the US Postal Service.

In January 1934, Tommy allegedly conspired to rob a postal vehicle, which nabbed a measly $4.00. He had been informed that the truck carried over $1,500 in cash and negotiable bonds. Instead, Tommy's two hired robbers only found four one-dollar bills in a pouch full of personal mail.

Tommy would later confide to fellow prison inmates that he suspected that the alleged amount was in the mail truck and money found was left to implicate him as part of the heist. Wick and Sandy were asked to locate the two thugs, but they were never found. That charge would later add two more years to his life sentence. Another utility office robbery was committed in central Kansas in 1933 and that too was attributed to Tommy. However, he escaped prosecution for that crime. Kansas Highway Patrol investigators tried to find sufficient evidence to implicate Tommy but could not get past unsubstantiated rumors and overzealous newspaper reporting.

It was Kansas detective Joe Anderson and Clint Miers, Assistant Chief of the KS State Crime Bureau, who decided that compiling enough evidence to indict and successfully prosecute Tommy would become their principal goal. Miers was considered the J. Edger Hoover of Kansas, and Anderson was an investigator known for his relentless pursuit of a criminal.

Their first big break came in 1934 when Ira Brackett and Glen Roy Wright were captured in Oklahoma and prosecuted for their part in the Kansas bank robberies involving a winch pickup. Wright, who already had murder charges against him, spent the rest of his life in the McAlester, Oklahoma Prison. Bracket was sentenced to 15 years at McAlester but was extradited a year later to Kansas at the insistence of Governor Alf Landon. Several years later, Brackett attempted to implicate Tommy as the leader of the robberies to get his sentence reduced. However, prosecutors lacked any specific proof beyond the safes excavated at Brackett's farm to indict Tommy beyond the crimes with which he was charged.

The next big break came in 1936 when Harry Campbell was captured and implicated Tommy in the Union Gas Robbery. Tommy, shrewd as ever, used as his defense that the two-year statutes of limitations of the 1930s had already passed and the fact that he was an Oklahoma resident at the time.

The trial for both Campbell and Tommy took place at the Montgomery County Courthouse in 1936, with Richard Becker serving as the prosecuting attorney. Becker was able to find 70 witnesses who testified that Tommy had a Coffeyville residence. For years, Tommy had kept a residence in both Southtown and Coffeyville, but his dual residency came back to haunt him. During his examination, Becker, every bit as crafty as his adversary, managed to coax out of Tommy, his former acquaintances with Alvin Karpis, Pretty Boy Floyd, Frank Nash, and Adam Richetti. Soon after the 1933 Union Station Massacre, federal agents had swooped through Southtown looking for Floyd and Richetti, who had been identified as part of the ambush outside the station. It is not known whether the two criminals were in Southtown at the time, but the agents did a thorough search of the town, including the Casa Del. The agents didn't find the criminals or the room behind the basement mirror. Richetti would later be caught, found guilty and executed. Floyd managed to escape a little longer but would be found on a farm outside Clarkston, Ohio and killed by federal agents led by Melvin Purvis.

Now Becker had something to work on to help solidify his prosecution. Tommy Hill, long known as a notorious criminal and considered by the Tulsa Tribune Newspaper as the "criminal overlord of Oklahoma." was starting to feel the pinch caused by his arrogance and carelessness. Another episode during the trial did not help his case during the proceedings. Colonel Wint Smith, an astute Kansas investigator who had helped the feds capture Alvin Karpis, was alerted of possible trouble during the trial when two strangers entered the courtroom. Smith directed troopers to photograph the men, later identified as Grover Burrhead Kready and John Brock, both Tulsa gamblers." This episode, though seemingly insignificant, was the final straw for the jurors. Becker asked that Tommy be sentenced to life imprisonment for his role as a habitual criminal, and he was convicted.

Tommy's sentence of life in prison as a "habitual criminal" was actually a statute at the time and gave Becker the tools he needed to put Tommy away, hopefully, forever. Today, the statute no longer exists due to potential civil rights and due process violations. However, by 1936, people were so fed up with the rampant crime that occurred so far during this decade that it is not surprising that Tommy lost his appeal and a year later went to prison in Lansing. He would remain incarcerated until 1943.

TOMMY AND HIS JAIL TIME

By the end of 1937, Tommy had lost his appeal to reduce the judge's sentence of life in prison, and he was facing a very long time in Lansing State Prison. To make matters worse, a federal court added two more years to Tommy's lifetime sentence over the $4 postal robbery from September 1934 in Coffeyville. However, by 1939, Tommy's situation in prison began to change.

First, then Kansas Governor Walter Huxman commuted Tommy's Life sentence to five years with time served. The Montgomery County District Attorney's office, now managed by the new district attorney, Clement Hall, vigorously protested, but the protest was to no avail. As soon as the announcement of the reduction in Tommy's sentence reached Coffeyville and Southtown, a rumor began that the governor had been paid for his actions. Even though this rumor has persisted for many years, there isn't any factual evidence to substantiate any claim of a payoff. The only unsubstantiated evidence of any payoff comes from Harold Haddan. Starting in the late 30's, he developed a close friendship with Wick, Madge, and their son Wes. He would frequently go to the Karn's home on the weekends for breakfast and take young Wes on fishing expeditions. During one of those breakfasts, Harold made a comment about Tommy's sentence reduction. Madge allegedly replied that she had to pay the governor $200,000 to get her brother's sentence reduced. Again, this is a story passed from father to son and by no means is a statement of fact. The only proof that can be given is that the story was passed on several times without any deviation. It will be up to the reader to draw his/her own conclusions.

At the time of the sentence reduction, Tommy went before a parole board and was denied because his paperwork had been replaced. With this denial, Tommy was transferred to the Kansas State Industrial Reformatory in Hutchinson for training. This transfer was unusual for the time. The Hutchinson prison was more of a reformatory school for young, non-violent felons sent there to be trained in a skill that could be used later after an inmate's release. Once at the reformatory, the warden quickly realized that Tommy was not only too old to be there but as a hardened criminal with a considerable record, his presence was more harmful to the young inmates than any good to himself. Within a matter of months, Tommy was sent back to Lansing.

During Tommy's time in prison, all was not well in his household. On January 14, 1940, Juletta Wolfe, Tommy's sister-in-law, was arrested with George Myers, an escaped convict from Missouri, on kidnapping charges in Oklahoma. According to the January 16 Miami Herald, J.G. Hail, a Commerce grocer, picked up Wolfe and Myers by the Route 66 bridge outside Miami and was promptly kidnapped at the point of a gun. The couple then drove Hill to Tahlequah, where his car broke down. After taking $25 from Hill, the couple put him on a train unharmed. When they were caught by county authorities, both admitted to the crime. Myers went back to prison in Missouri, and Wolfe was sentenced to a lengthy prison term. While looking for Wolfe, Nowata County authorities were able to determine that Tommy's wife had become estranged from him after he had gone to prison and was in the process of separating herself from his former illegal activities. Mrs. Hill continued to live in Southtown but struggled financially. Her final divorce from Tommy put her at odds with

Madge and Sammy, who refused to help support her. Financially destitute, she passed away within a year of Tommy being released in 1943.

While in Lansing, Tommy was a busy man. After returning to Lansing from Hutchinson, Tommy used his family contacts to obtain smuggled goods and drugs to sell to other inmates. The merchandise he sold was mainly toilet articles, which were hard to obtain inside the prison. He also sold small quantities of Marijuana and Benzedrine. The guards knew of Tommy's activities but usually kept quiet as long as they got a piece of any money that was transacted. However, several guards became disenchanted with their share and decided to punish him. In 1940, Tommy was accused of being involved in a narcotics ring within the prison. Due to a lack of hard evidence and what the warden considered a setup, the accusations against him were eventually dropped. In 1941, Tommy and Dr. S. A. Brainard, another inmate with a murder conviction, were accused of attempting to trap Robert Thomas, Lansing Machine Shop Superintendent for allegedly trying to selling them two ounces of cocaine. Again, the warden considered the charges a setup, but this time against Thomas. After an investigation, the charges were dropped, and Thomas was cleared of any wrongdoing. Based on news reports, Tommy spent his last two years of incarceration in relative calm. He probably knew of his pending release and chose to spend that time out of trouble.

THE TUNNELS IN SOUTHTOWN

One of the more intriguing aspects of Southtown's history is the tunnel system that was developed there. For some reason, tunneling was very popular prior to WWII, and

Southtown appeared to have numerous tunnels around the bars, several homes, and the Kansas/Oklahoma state line. The level of federal activity regarding illegal liquor sales beginning in the mid-1920s probably influenced their construction. One persistent story indicates that there were at least two or three leading from Oklahoma to Kansas. The tunnels were allegedly small, allowing only one person at a time to pass through. The ground Southtown sat on was dirt that was primarily clay-like in its composition. It was the kind of dirt that was ideally suited for making bricks. However, the dirt tended to shift when the ground was wet. This condition forced the tunnels to be about three feet below the surface and only four or five feet in height. Lighting was probably provided by large flashlights used by the people traveling through the tunnels. When this book project started, considerable effort was made to determine if these tunnels existed. Happily, two eyewitnesses have come forth stating that they either walked through a tunnel or at least attempted to but were stopped by the tunnel's poor condition. Here are the facts. First, there was a tunnel from Sandy Hill's home on Wyandotte Street to the Southern Club on the old main highway. It was used in the30s through the late 50s and is probably still in existence today to some degree. It was in this tunnel that one of the eyewitnesses claimed that her grandparents hid Pretty Boy Floyd when Oklahoma deputies and federal marshals were in the area searching for him. Since Oklahoma county deputies and federal marshals were actively searching for Floyd around Southtown in early 1932, there is a very high probability that this story is true. Floyd was known to be in the area around this time, and he would naturally go to Tommy, Wick or Sandy for a place to hide.

Since this tunnel was small and dug out of wet clay, Floyd probably stayed there no more than a few days before heading east through Missouri. The second tunnel ran from the Southern Club to the gas station just south of the state line. This tunnel was allegedly used primarily for transporting liquor between both locations. A third tunnel ran from a house across from the grocery store but evidently stopped short of the home's property line. This tunnel was probably dug by the grocer to transport liquor but for some reason, was never completed. In addition, there were probably other tunnels that existed, but there is no documentation to prove their existence.

The first tunnel is the one that allegedly ran from the Tavern bar across the road to the Kansas side. This tunnel would have run a short distance, probably less than 60 feet, to the Kansas side of the state line road right next to either the second or third Tavern building. This tunnel would have been used by tavern employees or customers wanting a quick exit to the Kansas side of the state line to avoid being arrested. In the early 60's, US 160 was moved to the west of the original road that ran through town. Its path ran directly through the Tavern's location which resulted in the three structures being demolished. The new road has a large drainage ditch on its west side and if a tunnel existed, it would have been gone for over 60 years.

The second alleged tunnel ran south to the state line from the Casa Del. Again; there is no proof of this tunnel, but a former Southtown resident recently found a small hole just north of the state line and is attempting to put a flexible camera in the hole to see if it is part of a tunnel. Like the alleged Tavern tunnel, this one would also been used for a quick and quiet escape to Kansas.

The third and most intriguing tunnel allegedly ran from the Casa Del to Tommy's home on Wyandotte Street, with a branch running to Madge and Wick's home. Although there isn't any physical proof of this tunnel, there are indications of its existence. First, since the Casa Del had a basement with a secret room behind a revolving mirror, a tunnel from that room would have made sense if it were going to run 400 to 500 feet to Tommy's home. A tunnel branch also makes sense because it would have run under Madge and Wick's front yard to Tommy's basement. Several credible stories come from a Coffeyville resident who claims to have known about the tunnel to Tommy's home. Another Coffeyville resident shared a credible story that money made from the Casa Del would be transported to the Karn's basement via the tunnel and counted by the wives of their employees.

Thus, the tunnel stories are credible. Two eyewitnesses and several stories have been verified by at least two present and former Southtown residents.

CHAPTER 7
INCREASED STATE AND LOCAL LAW ENFORCEMENT CAUSES SOUTHTOWN TO SUFFER IN THE LATE 1930S AND EARLY 1940S

With Tommy in prison and completely out of business as far as his criminal activities were concerned, running Southtown and keeping the various bar owners in line became the responsibility of the Karns and the remaining Hills.

After the 12-month bar closings ended in 1930, federal liquor agents continued to monitor the town's liquor activities. However, in 1933, President Roosevelt successfully repealed the Volstead Act and legalized selling and serving alcohol at the federal level. This repeal also ended federal intervention at the state and local levels. One provision of the repeal was putting the legalization and enforcement of alcohol sales at the state level. Each state would be able to determine the level of legalized alcohol within its own borders. Many states went a step further and allowed counties to determine the level of legal alcohol sales their citizens wanted. Some states like Kansas and Oklahoma decided to stay dry allowing only the sale of 3.2 beer.

Thus, even with the repeal of the Volstead Act, Coffeyville and Southtown were still located in dry states and had to deal with state and county anti-liquor enforcers. Southtown suffered particularly. Oklahoma, by then, had a bureau of investigation, a Nowata County Sheriff's office, and a District Judge who was committed to putting a clamp on Southtown's illegal booze and gambling activities.

Starting in 1935, a series of bar closures began. Judge W.A. Thomason ordered the closure and padlocking of the Casa Del, Silver Slipper, and Nut House clubs. Normally a closure could last for several weeks and up to several months. But, since Southtown had other bars that would remain open, like the Southern Club, Hi-Ho Club, Bumps, and other smaller clubs, business in Southtown continued.

The closures were effective for small periods of time. Because of the court order, the Nut House and the Silver Slipper closed for an extended period for lack of business. The closures probably gave Judge Thomason a sense of success because he laid off ordering raids for a while. All he did was give the owners of the closed bars a chance either to regroup and open or to sell their establishment to another proprietor.

In 1939, Judge Thomason was at it again with more raids and closures. The raids happened at peak times of the year, usually New Year's Eve. The Nowata Daily Star reported in both January 1941 and 1942 of raids and closures of the Casa Del Club. Obviously, Judge Thomason and the current Nowata County District Attorney were focusing on Wick Karns and the club. The rationale was probably that if the largest and busiest club could be periodically closed, the others might take notice and watch their illegal activities. However, something much bigger was occurring in Montgomery and

Labette Counties that even the diligent judge from Nowata County couldn't stop.

WORLD WAR II AND A SECOND BOOM FOR SOUTHTOWN

World War II for the United States began with the December 7, 1941, Japanese attack on Pearl Harbor and subsequent declarations of war between America and the Axis countries of Japan, Germany, and Italy. With the declaration of war and the country in full mobilization, US Army Air Force training bases and ammunition plants quickly rose across the country. Montgomery County would gain two air force training bases with a total of close to 10,000 personnel, and Labette County would build an army ammunition plant just outside of Parsons that, upon completion, would employ 10,000 people. In fact, Southeast Kansas was in the midst of a military boom, and there were a lot of soldiers and ammunition plant workers looking for places to party. Southtown was back in business again.

By the end of 1942, Montgomery County, two Army Air Force training bases and auxiliary airfields were nearing completion, and Labette County was close to finishing one of the two ammunition plants to be located in Kansas. By early to mid-1943, both bases and the ammunition plant were complete enough to begin housing soldiers and plant employees. By late 1943, the training bases near Coffeyville and Independence had a military complement of 5,300 soldiers each. The ammunition plant employed had over 4,000 government employees so far, and the numbers were growing rapidly. At this point, the Army had brought in soldiers to guard the facility. In Parsons, the housing shortage was so great that barracks and homes would be built to house the overflow. The regional railroads and Interurban trolley system were being taxed to maximum effort.

With such a swell of both civilians and soldiers, there had to be a place or places to accommodate the desire for entertainment. Coffeyville, for its part, had South Walnut Street with its numerous bars and other forms of entertainment, mainly prostitution, on the second floors of several buildings. Several elderly Coffeyville residents shared that South Walnut on Friday and especially Saturday night were wild with soldiers on leave. But since Coffeyville could serve only 3.2 beer and had a police chief determined to keep downtown civil, many soldiers and civilians made their way down to Southtown for the extra excitement it could offer. The Casa Del, Tavern, Hi Ho Club, Bumps, Southern Club, and the Silver Slipper were serving both soldiers and civilians at full capacity. On any weekend evening, as many as 800 to 1,000 soldiers from the Coffeyville and Independence air bases would travel to Southtown to get drunk and hopefully find a woman to party with. Surprisingly, the Nowata Sheriff's office was strangely silent. Only one major raid was recorded in 1943, shortly after Tommy was released from Lansang. Like before, Tommy, Wick, and Sandy were arrested for serving illegal liquor. But none of the defendants served any meaningful time in jail and this fact allowed business in Southtown to go on as usual. Wartime business would continue to bustle without any further publicized incidents.

SOUTHTOWN IS THE PLACE TO BE FOR AREA SOLDIERS

By April 1943, Montgomery County was filling up with soldiers who volunteered to be trained as pilots. They were young, single men with all of the energy and weaknesses someone their age possessed. They were paid well, had room and board, and clothing provided. They also had money to spend on the vices Southtown provided.

The Coffeyville base was several miles outside of town, with a special road built to take army personnel to and from US 169. Because of the business and potential profit available, Coffeyville transit buses ran a regular route to and from the base. Once in town, soldiers could stay and play on South Walnut or if they were more adventurous, take the trolley to Southtown for an ever-greater adventure. Once in Southtown, soldiers had access to beer, liquor, gambling and prostitutes. A good time was readily available while the money lasted.

The same was true for the air base in Independence. Located six miles from the city limits, the air base there was fortunate in that it was only half a mile from the Interurban trolley line to Coffeyville and Southtown. Soldiers could ride the trolley all the way to Southtown, have fun, and, if they were smart, catch the last run to Independence before it stopped for the night. The ones who were too drunk to make the evening connection could ride the next day and hopefully not be considered Absent Without Leave (AWOL). For the soldiers who did not make it back in time to their base, a stockade with a small building and barbed wire fence was waiting for them.

The people who worked at the Parsons Ammunition Plant were a slightly different story. With almost 10,000 men and women working at the plant, only a small portion lived in Parsons. The town never grew more than 12,000 residents, even during WWII. People from all over Southeast Kansas worked at the ammunition plant. The ones who lived in Cherokee and Crawford Counties probably went to Joplin for their drinking and recreation. As for Labette and Montgomery Counties, plant workers from those areas probably chose Southtown for their ultimate fun. The Interurban, a 1912 marvel, ran from Parsons to Southtown on a regular schedule. Plant workers who lived a reasonable distance from an Interurban stop could use its inexpensive services to travel to Southtown. Cherryvale, located between Coffeyville and Parsons, had a double benefit. It had not only the Interurban line but also a "Doodlebug" mini train that ran from its Santa Fe station directly to downtown Coffeyville. Despite wartime rationing, Southtown was in the middle of a transportation "perfect storm." Anyone from Montgomery or Labette County had some mode of transportation available to them to make the trek to and from Southtown.

TROUBLE FROM TULSA

Although Tulsa was technically a dry city and county in the 40s, illegal liquor could be had depending on a person's connections. Outside of a Black dance hall on Apache Street, places to drink and dance were limited for Whites in Tulsa. As a result, young Tulsans, mostly thugs and other troublemakers, would make the 70-mile journey to Southtown to get drunk and chase women. It was the most exciting place to party in northeast Oklahoma and close enough to travel. On any given weekend evening, at least 50 to 100 young Tulsans would visit Southtown to party. Under normal circumstances, their presence should not have been much of a problem. However, occasional fights would occur between Soldiers and young Tulsans. The problem was not the fights themselves but what happened afterward.

While serving as Mayor of Coffeyville, the author would periodically visit the town's police chief to learn if there were any potential problems his department was experiencing. On one occasion, he shared several incidents near Southtown where there were outdoor parties in a field near the Oklahoma state line. On these occasions, a fight would break out between a local person and a Tulsa thug over a girl. Later, the local person would be found dead lying neatly over the Missouri Pacific railroad tracks cut in half by a train. Several of these incidents occurred in the mid-1980s, but the police chief told of similar deaths that occurred going back to the early 1940's when Southtown was full of partying soldiers. He specifically remembered two accidents around 1944 when a soldier was found the next day dead on a railroad track neatly cut into two pieces. The Coffeyville and Nowata newspapers were never notified, and without any witnesses, the investigations would quietly end. The air base commandant would simply report that the deceased soldier died during training exercises.

When Tommy returned from prison, he decided that it was time to end the railroad deaths and quickly put his men to work. By the end of 1944, fighting between Tulsans and soldiers had been eliminated. Any disputes between Tommy and a Tulsan usually concluded with a rap on the back of the Thug's Head With His Blackjack.

TOMMY IS RELEASED, AND A NEW ERA BEGINS FOR SOUTHTOWN

In March 1943, Tommy Hill was released from Lansing State Prison on probation after five years of incarceration. Tommy was 48 years old and a smarter man compared to the time when his legal problems began. The gangster era was over, and bank robbing was no longer a national pastime for criminals. World War II caused the United States to fight on two fronts at opposite places in the World. The nation became fully mobilized and created a huge increase in economic output across the country.

The wartime boom was the environment Tommy stepped into when he was released. Business was booming in Southtown, and Tommy wanted to return to his former position. But one endeavor he avoided was returning to robbing banks, utility companies and postal trucks. Although small-town bank robberies would continue clearly into the 2020s, the golden age of bank robbing was gone. Dillinger, Floyd, the Barkers, Baby Face Nelson, Bonnie and Clyde and many others were dead, and Alvin Karpis and other bank robbers were sitting in Alcatraz or some other state or federal prison. Tommy had served his time, but before 1943 would end, he and Wick would be arrested again by the Nowata County Sheriff's office for selling illegal liquor. They were lucky and served only six months in the county jail. Until his death in 1953, Tommy was never caught or prosecuted again.

Not wanting to go back to prison, Tommy returned to something that made him money in his 20s and early 30s, hiding criminals. This time, he used another approach and hid only criminals from outside Oklahoma who would pay very well. To accomplish this goal, Tommy purchased a newer airplane that would hold more than two passengers, and he renewed his contacts with the various Chicago organized crime families. For the Chicago families, it was a win-win situation. When one of their members got too hot, Tommy flew in and transported him back to Southtown without the FBI knowing it. Hot Springs was no longer the safe haven it once was; Southtown was perfect. Even though the FBI was aware of Southtown and its numerous illegal activities, J. Edger Hoover considered it too small to bother. By the mid-40s, the FBI replaced the Treasury Department as the premier law enforcement agency in America. During World War II, his agency spent most of its energy tracking down German and Japanese saboteurs. Once the war ended, Hoover concentrated primarily on the high-profile cases of Communists in America. Southtown was left to the state and county agencies still interested in chasing bootleg liquor and gambling.

This gap in federal and state enforcement of Southtown was perfect for Tommy. After renewing his Chicago contacts, Tommy approached EC Mullendore about hiding criminals at his ranch. In the 1940s, The Mullendore Ranch, located west of Bartlesville, was one of the largest in Oklahoma. With its vast acreage and large herds of cattle, EC was always looking for financing. After his tragic murder in the early 70s, EC was thought to have been in deep debt with the mafia. Although never proven, there is one fact that was learned from an eyewitness and participant. By early 1945, Tommy had made a deal with EC to hide criminals on the run at his ranch.

One story that was told about this era was from an elderly woman who was involved with Tommy transporting criminals to and from Southtown and the Mullendore Ranch.

Maryanne Privitt was born in Southtown to a well-known family. They were not rich but always worked hard. Maryanne, a spunky girl with a strong work ethic, was looking for a job as a teenager in the middle of World War II in a town where a lot of soldiers were blowing their paychecks. Maryanne could have cared less about the bars and certainly wasn't scared of a bunch of drunk soldiers. She had grown up in a rough town and knew how to handle herself.

When Tommy returned and was ready to start his new business hiding criminals at the ranch, he needed a dependable driver to take these hardened characters to the ranch and back. Tommy knew of Maryanne's family and their ability to be discrete. He needed someone who could be trusted to keep his or her mouth shut and not be afraid of the passengers. Maryanne fit the bill. She was trustworthy, a good driver and had just enough sass to keep most men in their place. Maryanne was hired and quickly put to work. Tommy flew the criminals in from Chicago and upon landing, were met by Maryanne and quickly driven away. Tommy wanted them out of Southtown as soon as possible. He also warned his new guests to keep their hands off Maryanne or suffer the consequences of being killed or beaten and left in the middle of nowhere. The criminals were also reminded that being dropped off at a police station to be arrested was an option if Maryanne was harassed. During her trips, Maryanne was never physically or verbally abused by the men she was transporting. One comment she made later was how tanned and physically fit the hiding criminals looked when picked up for their return trip home. EC's ranch foreman must have worked them hard during their stay. Maryanne performed these services for several years before deciding to move to Coffeyville and put her excellent bookkeeping skills to work. She later went to college and earned a graduate degree in education before starting a career as a college business instructor and grant director before retiring.

CHAPTER 8
WORLD WAR II ENDS

By early 1945, the War and its end were evident. Germany was on its heels, losing men and ground from two fronts, and Japan had virtually lost most of its navy, leaving the country vulnerable to an imminent invasion by US forces. As a result, the training bases in Coffeyville and Independence started to wind down their operations. By the summer of that year, both bases were on the verge of being closed. This fact left Southtown with a lot less business. However, when one opportunity leaves, another can rise, and this was the case in Southtown, too.

At the end of World War II, Coffeyville was probably the strongest economically since the first economic surge in 1904. The community still had two refineries, a smelter, several foundries and numerous smaller companies. The downtown sector was also experiencing a boom, easily recovering from the war's rationing days. Coffeyville was doing so well it built a new hospital and started the process of replacing its old and outdated elementary schools. It had a population of over 19,000 during the late 40's and boasted the lowest personal taxes in Kansas. Unfortunately, Coffeyville was smug with its success, and the town became blind to what it would need to continue to grow. After the 1943 flood, which inundated the Sinclair Refinery, CEO Harry Sinclair asked the city council to build a levy to prevent future flooding. The council refused, and Sinclair submitted a second request offering to relocate his company's pipeline headquarters from Independence to Coffeyville. The Coffeyville City Commission refused again, and Sinclar closed the refinery. The Coffeyville City Clerk recorded Sinclair's final comments. Sinclair was so angry with his former town that he vowed to live to see grass grow in the streets of Coffeyville.

Another large company that produced leather products wanted to move to Coffeyville and supply the town with numerous jobs. Not wanting a "stinky factory" in town, the city council also refused to approve its zoning request. Despite these two incidents, Coffeyville would remain a prosperous community for the next 25 years.

As for Southtown, business was good. Veterans either returning home or moving to Coffeyville filled the void left by Army Air Corps base closures and lack of soldiers. On Friday and Saturday evenings, the gas station on the Oklahoma side of US 169 had a line of cars reaching the Onion Creek bridge with thirsty drivers wanting to purchase package liquor. This line would remain until 1948, when Kansas repealed its prohibition laws.

The clubs were also booming with bootleg liquor, dancing and gambling. Many of the clubs began offering evening meals and live music, hoping to entice area couples to spend their weekend evenings drinking, dining, dancing, and gambling.

The new approach worked so well that Tommy decided to curtail his business of hiding criminals on the run.

There were good reasons for moving away from this enterprise. After the 1946 Havana Conference, the US Mafia made big strides to equally distribute crime family turf and avoid needless killings and wars. Except for the killings of Bugsy Seigel and Kansas City Crime Boss Charles Binaggio, mafia hits and gangster murders dropped significantly. There was no need to hide mafia-hit men on the Mullendore Ranch. Another good reason for ending this part of his business was that beginning in 1947 and through 1951, the Nowata Sheriff's office and Oklahoma agents were relentlessly obtaining warrants to search Southtown clubs for illegal liquor and gambling. Most of the raids produced not only large stashes of illegal liquor but also gambling chips, dice, several roulette wheels, and in one case, an expensive oak table for crap games.

Sandy was the usual victim of these searches, and his Southern Club was hit to the point it was closed by 1950 and would not open again until 1969. Even the Casa Del was normally included in the warrants but managed to keep its doors open. With the amount of legal pressure from state and county authorities, Tommy and Sandy chose to cooperate and resume operations as soon as possible. Neither wanted to be caught in an illegal incident that would put them back in the Nowata County Jail.

ENTER A NEW GUY, BOB FOLK

Around 1946, a new guy moved into Southtown and quickly attached himself to the Hills and the Karns. Bob Folk was a short, stocky person in his early 20s and a northeast Oklahoma native. Wick Karns was the first to notice that this new kid had a raw talent with cards and dice. He took the kid and decided to turn him into a gambler with exceptional skill.

Bob did not disappoint him. Along with his other obvious gambling talents, Bob also excelled at the roulette tables.

For starters, Wick and Sandy decided to employ Bob at the state line gas station with two tasks in mind. First, Bob was to oversee the sale of packaged liquor at the station and manage the long line of cars from Coffeyville on the weekends. His next task was to set up poker and crap games on the second floor of the gas station building. Wick would provide Bob with the funds he would need to start the game and afterward split the profits. In time, Bob would win enough money to provide his own seed money and keep more of the winnings himself.

When Kansas repealed its prohibition laws in late 1948, and the line of cars began to diminish, Bob moved to the Casa Del and eventually oversaw that club's activities, including the sporadic poker games in the basement.

With the amount of legal pressure coming from Nowata County and the State of Oklahoma on the smaller clubs, the Casa Del, with Tommy, Sandy and the Karns money to support it become the primary venue for eating, drinking and dancing. Bob's gambling activities would, for a time remain on the gas station's second floor. He would also rent a house on the south side of town next to the Hi Ho Club, and he set up games there. With the house, he could offer poker and craps with more space. The house wasn't much to look at but had plenty of cars parked in front of it on most evenings. Fortunately for Bob, Nowata County left him alone. During a phone interview, George Elliott, a Southtown resident who has lived there since his birth in the early 1940s, divulged that the Sheriff was paid $300 a month to leave Bob alone. There is no proof of this arrangement, but the fact he didn't interfere most of the time is at least interesting.

With money flowing in Coffeyville and jobs easy to get, a lot of wanna-be gamblers came to the surface. Most of these suckers were men who had grown up poor during the Great Depression and then went off to fight the Germans or Japanese in the early 40s. Most of these men who served overseas had been gone for several years. They had money accumulated and, upon returning, wanted to blow some steam and get the war and its horrible memories behind them. Many joined either the VFW or American Legion, and when Kansas prohibition ended in 1948, they could get a mixed drink at one of the clubs. The drinking and comradery were fine, and some clubs would open a room for some small-stakes' poker. This level of activity worked okay for a veteran who wanted a fun and ,small-stakes game. However, with Southtown and its higher stakes and a wider variety of games like craps and roulette, the bigger gamblers headed there.

Not all gamblers were veterans. Many were prominent local businessmen who thought they were good enough to beat the games south of the state line. They were wrong. Wick and Sandy hired experienced people to run their house games. These dealers came from all over the region. Some had been involved in the secret games local mob bosses ran in Kansas City, St. Louis, and even Tulsa. Others, like Bob, were naturals who had that special God-given skill to win, regardless of the opponents or stakes. Of the club players, Bob was the best. He knew when to hold and when to fold. Bob was also a master at crap games. He had a great dice arm and knew how to spread his money and beat the odds.

Bob also had the perfect poker face. His opponents could never read him.

It was around the late 40s and early 50s when Bob's reputation developed. Harold Haddan spoke occasionally of Coffeyville businessmen and entrepreneurs going to Southtown and losing their shirts trying to beat Bob. One businessman lost his investment in a local grain elevator in a poker game. Others lost their cars or family jewelry to Bob. At one point, Bob had won enough cars from poker games that he opened a small used car sales lot just south of the old theater. George Elliot spoke at length about the number of different cars Bob was always driving. The car business was fun for a while, but Bob had bigger plans in mind for Southtown and for himself.

CHANGES COME TO SOUTHTOWN AND COFFEYVILLE

As the late 40s and early 50s wore on, the Karns and Hills decided it was time to sit back and keep a lower profile. By the early 50s, Tommy had remarried a local elementary school teacher and was living a quieter life. His new wife, Velma, was very popular and highly respected. She gave Tommy the kind of personal stability he had lacked since moving to Southtown. They were a happy couple, and he regularly attended school functions where Velma was involved. It was also around this time that Tommy's health started to decline. Sandy also had started to develop some health issues and would be found in bed most of the time. Wick and Madge were in their sixties, and both wanted less stress and public notoriety. Madge had started the process of cleansing her image from the early 30s and 20 years later, she was considered the matriarch of Southtown. Both Tommy and Wick had built new homes in the early 50s and installed a tunnel from the Casa Del to their basements. The homes were very nice but subdued. Madge had developed a reputation as a person always willing to h elp someone in need and nobody in Southtown wanted to jeopardize her generosity. Wick had also settled down to being a quiet investor dabbling in livestock and mineral leases. Because of their growing health issues, Tommy and Sandy also took several steps back and tried to enjoy what was left of their lives.

With the changes in the old guard, Bob quietly appeared as the new leader in town. He had the money and connections to start the process of taking over Southtown.

However, Bob's ascension to the informal role as boss of Southtown was gradual. State and county liquor enforcement authorities continued to be a thorn in Southtown's side. From 1947 to 1951, Oklahoma liquor control agents and the Nowata County Sheriff's Office conducted a series of raids. The most prominent were raids in late 1947, 1949 and 1951. All were conducted at the end of the year when people were more prone to partying. In all three cases, a substantial amount of illegal liquor and gambling items were found. The pressure was so bad on the Southern Club it ceased business. The other clubs, including the Casa Del, also suffered. But despite the raids, most of the clubs remained open, usually restocking their liquor, gambling chips and dice in a matter of days. Even with prohibition ending in Kansas in 1948, Southtown continued as the destination point for good food, liquor, dancing and gambling. The clubs even advertised in local newspapers to try to attract more people. If there was ever a time that Southtown deserved its notorious reputation, the 40s and 50s were it.

CHAPTER 9
DEATH IN SOUTHTOWN

On September 11, 1953, Tommy Hill passed away at the Coffeyville Memorial Hospital. He had been admitted several days earlier. Tommy's death was unexpected, and all of Southtown mourned. He was quietly buried at the Grandview Cemetery in Coffeyville.

Surprisingly, most of the area newspapers gave Tommy's death considerable coverage. They wrote about many of his exploits and even printed a 1937 Tulsa Tribune Newspaper quote stating that in the 30s, Tommy was considered the "crime overlord of the South."

Before the year ended, Tommy's brother Sandy passed away. He was only 43 but had left his mark in Southtown. Madge and Wick would inherit both Tommy and Sandy's interest in the town's clubs and their activities. Within a few years, Bob would have control of these interests.

MOVING ON FROM TOMMY'S LEGACY

By 1954, Madge and Wick were ready to move away from Southtown's notorious activities. Bob had been planning for years to purchase the Casa Del and the Karn's other club's interests. By 1955, Bob was the principal mover and shaker in Southtown. Unlike Tommy, Bob was a quiet person who kept his personal life and business interests very much to himself. High profiles usually attract the attention of law enforcement agencies. A classic example that created a lot of news publicity was the shooting death of Bugsy Siegel in his Los Angeles home. His extravagant lifestyle in Southern California and involvement in the construction of the Las Vegas Tropicana resort were always in the news. In the end, Bugsy was killed. Bob took this lesson to heart for the remainder of his life; he successfully kept a low profile.

In the 1950s, some of the old bars started to close. The Southern Club had been closed by the early 50s and the Nut House, a dive for years, finally locked its doors. The Tavern, Bumps, and the Hi-Ho Club were still active, but they were gone by 1960.

There were other places still active. Pete and Kelly's, a cafe and bar, was popular and would remain open into the 1980s. The Silver Slipper, behind the Hi-Ho Club, was purchased by Bob and turned into a bingo parlor. A new café, which served great food and beer, opened in a converted army barracks building. It was called Bones Café and would stay in business past 2000.

Of all the places, new and old, the one that gave Southtown its notorious reputation was the Casa Del. When it came to going to Southtown for drinking and dancing, the Casa Del was by far the most popular entertainment spot. Even though the building was showing its age, the Casa Del would remain popular until it closed in 1959.

PARTY TIME AND DEATH COMES TO BOTH SOUTHTOWN AND COFFEYVILLE.

By the mid-50s, South Walnut was the wild spot in Coffeyville. There were at least seven bars between 9th and

11th streets. The Coffeyville Police would have no less than two officers walking the South Walnut beat on most evenings. Even though the beer was only 3.2, men would go in and drink to the point of drunkenness. In later years, former Coffeyville police officers would tell stories of how they would walk down Walnut and look for the noisiest bars. They would then go in, pick out the loudest drunk and knock him down with their nightsticks. The officers would then drag the unconscious drunk by his collar down Walnut to the police station on 7th Street. This activity was their way of letting the other drunks on Walnut know that they could be next.

Another unique and popular bar located in Coffeyville was the Skyline Dance Hall. It was located on private land atop Coffeyville's "Big Hill" next to Pfiester Park. It resembled a converted army barracks. The Skyline was a popular place until constant fighting there caused it to be closed in the late 50s.

Around the early 50s, an avenue for purchasing illegal liquor for local college students and minors opened. In the then Black side of town on 5th street, a gentleman confined to a wheelchair started selling liquor out of his house. His name was "Cripple Sam." Underage men and women went to his house, selected a bottle, paid and quickly left. The transactions normally occurred in the evening after dark. The street was poorly lit and ideal for a group of teenagers to slip in and discreetly buy their illegal booze. The liquor allegedly came from Southtown because the bottles didn't have the Kansas tax label used at that time.

Some firsthand accounts of this era exist. In the mid-50s, Jack Cody was a strapping 15-year-old lad who liked to fight.

He was large and looked older than he was. Jack had learned to box at the Coffeyville Boys Club and eventually trained for Golden Gloves matches. Around 1955, Jack managed to get into the Hi Ho Club but was confronted by its bouncer, JD King. King was a big fellow who liked to use a blackjack and hit his adversaries from behind. Jack was one of his victims. One evening Jack and a friend went to the Hi Ho Club for an evening of drinking and fun. As the evening wore on, both got a little drunk and loud. King, knowing that Jack and his friend were only in their mid-teens, decided to kick them out. Using his usual tactic of hitting from behind, King picked Jack, who was the larger of the two and hit him from behind with his blackjack. Jack was knocked to the floor and dragged out of the club. When Jack tried to get up and enter, King shot at his feet with a .410 shotgun. Jack vowed revenge.

Several nights later, Jack caught up with King and his brother at the Skyline Dance Hall and confronted him. Quick with his fists, Jack knocked King down and out with two punches.

A short time after that, King was back at the Hi Ho Club bouncing. One evening, Clinton Little, a local, was at the club and got into an argument with King. Little, aware of King's hit-from-behind tactics, forced the bouncer to a frontal confrontation. The argument and resulting fistfight started on the dance floor and continued after Little knocked King through the front door into the parking lot. Unable to control his anger, Little went to his car and pulled out a revolver with hollow points. He shot King three times in the chest, and King died a short time later at the Coffeyville Memorial Hospital Emergency Room. Little was arrested by Nowata County authorities and tried for murder. Little was fortunate. His family hired a good attorney who got him off on a technicality. King's friends vowed revenge, but Little left Southtown and remained away until tempers settled. The King incident put a stain of death on Southtown and only added to its reputation for violence. The town would never be the same.

BIG CHANGES FOR SOUTHTOWN

In 1958, Bob built a modern motel between the closed Southern Club and the aging Tavern location. Two years later, US 169 would be relocated west, causing even further changes. It is interesting to note that the motel's layout exactly met the contours of the new road that was built two years later. Evidently, Bob had some inside information on the new highway.

In 1959, Oklahoma had a special election and repealed its prohibition laws of 1907. The new law provided for Class B bars where the patron brought his own liquor bottle, and the bar provided the mixers. Other changes included selling beer in bars and grocery stores. Liquor stores were allowed to open, but only warm beer was allowed to be sold in those locations.

One benefit for Southtown was that it could legally sell beer on Sundays while Coffeyville was dry that day.

Southtown ignored the Class B license requirements and continued to sell liquor by the drink. With the new liquor law, there were good and bad. The good was that Oklahoma had finally got its head out of the sand and was slowly moving towards a more reasonable drinking environment. The bad was that Southtown had lost its lure as a notorious place to party.

SOUTHTOWN AND THE 60S

By 1960, major changes were occurring in Southtown. First, the Casa Del closed for good and was replaced by the Southern Supper Club in the former Hi-Ho building. Bob had the new club completely remodeled and turned it into a restaurant with great food and a large wet bar. The dancing area was turned into a place for parties and banquets. Bob had started to tame Southtown.

Another big change was the relocation of US 169 west of Main Street. Because the new highway went right through the old Tavern location, it was demolished. With the new highway, the old gas station south of the state line was also demolished, and later, the property was turned into a residence. The old Casa Del was sold to a local resident, demolished and converted into a residence.

By the early 1960s, Southtown was subdued. Except for Pete and Kelly's Café and Bar, all the other clubs had closed. Gambling, now controlled by Bob, was limited to games at the motel or on the second floor of his new club. By this time, Bob had the reputation of an experienced gambler, and he alone controlled when and where the games took place. Gone were sleazy bars and makeshift games resembling saloons of the past century. Also gone were Tommy's hanger and landing strip. Bob purchased both properties and turned the hanger into the South Coffeyville Stockyards. Since the Jensen family owned another landing strip and hanger west of town, Bob turned the land back to agricultural uses.

By the mid-1960s, Southtown has become Bob's town. He was also constantly looking for bigger and better investments. Bob was alleged to have been an early investor in the Las Vegas Caesar's Palace. From the late sixties on, Bob began to offer junkets to Las Vegas for fun and gambling. He offered a free weekend, including free airfare, room and meals if the participants agreed to spend at least $800 in gambling money. The gambling requirements were small by today's standards. But taking the mid-60s economy into consideration, $800 at that time was a large sum of money.

THE 1970S AND FORWARD

In the 1970s, Southtown and its notorious days had become a memory of days gone by. The same can be said of Coffeyville. The Urban Renewal program virtually eliminated South Walnut from the alley south of Weinberg's Western Wear to 11th Street. Gone were the bars on that street. There would be other bars, like Jiggs on 4th Street ,which lasted until 2018, and Weber's on East 4th Street, primarily serving Blacks. Weber's Bar and the violence associated with it would become so bad that by 1980, it would be declined a beer license by the Coffeyville City Commission. Without a beer license, the bar was closed. There was a third notorious bar in Coffeyville that, despite its violent reputation, would last until the COVID-19 pandemic closed it. It was called the Stockman's Bar and was located just south of the Coffeyville Stockyards. Now, it is nothing more than a vacant lot.

A person driving through Coffeyville in 2023 would notice that the town lacks bars and clubs. In 1970, there were 23 bars in Coffeyville, and now there are none except what is in a few restaurants. Even Jiggs finally closed and is now a smoke shop.

A FEW BRIGHT LIGHTS BEFORE CONCLUDING

In the 1970s and 80s, Southtown was still an active community. Bones Café was open and usually busy every evening. The Southern Supper Club, with its excellent food and open bar, was the premier place to eat and drink until the early 2000s. During this period, the Southern Supper Club was considered the best place to eat and drink for area residents. Harold Haddan, the longtime local photographer, had secured the contract to photograph the Field Kindley High School Junior-Senior Prom since the early 70s, and he noted by the early 80s that many high school participants would get decked out and go to the Southern Supper Club. They would travel in a stretch limousine to the club and get drunk. By the time these students arrived at the prom, they were sloshed. Harold would ask some of them where they had been, and the answer was always the Southern Supper Club. No blame was attached to Bob. By the 70s, he was hiring managers to run his club business. He had bigger fish to catch. If there was any blame, it would have to go to the club's manager. Another interesting note on the Southern Supper Club was that until Oklahoma vastly updated its liquor laws in 1985, the club constantly maintained an illegal wet bar. The Oklahoma liquor authorities would come to the club about once a year, close the bar and confiscate the liquor. The wet bar was usually open for business again in a few days. After 1985, the Southern Supper Club no longer had to worry about an illegal wet bar. From that time on, all Bob had to do was apply for a legal liquor license. Again, Southtown's notorious reputation was buried even further.

GAMBLING IN SOUTHOWN BEFORE THE FINAL CURTAIN

Even though Southtown was transforming from a wild town to a bedroom community for Coffeyville residents tired of paying high vehicle taxes, gambling continued. By the mid to late 60s, Bob was the "king "of Southtown." Madge and Wick had quietly gone into retirement, and their son, Wes, was living in Texas. The Southern Supper Club, with its fine food, banquet facilities, and open wet bar was the place to go for business meetings over drinks or a date night for couples. Bob expanded his holdings by opening the South Coffeyville Stockyards across the road from his supper club. The stockyards facility was a great move in that it brought area ranchers to town to deal in livestock and finish the day at the supper club across the street. It was also a time for Bob to engage in some poker or craps with ranchers flushed with money.

There has been a persistent rumor that Bob was one of the original investors in Caesars Palace. He might have purchased some stock in the place, but there isn't any evidence that Bob was a major investor.

When the 70s began, Coffeyville had approved its destructive urban renewal project and more than doubled the production capacity of its electric power plant. The town also built a new water treatment plant designed to accommodate a community of 25,000. There was a brief discussion about expanding the Verdigris River navigation project from the Port of Catoosa to Coffeyville, but the cost versus potential future revenue eventually killed the proposal. Even with this project gone, Coffeyville was still poised for growth. New industries were located at the town's industrial park, and current companies, like Funk Manufacturing, were expanding and adding more workers.

During this period of expansion in Coffeyville, Bob had become a larger-than-life figure who was a gambler second to none and flush with money. He played for high stakes and Coffeyville's prominent businessmen constantly lost playing against him. By this time, Bob had purchased a ranch close to Lenapah, off US169. On this land, Bob built a large, beautiful ranch home that could be easily seen from the highway. It was here that Bob would have regular evenings of high-stakes gambling. By this time, Bob had a reputation as a gambler who seldom lost but had a line of people wanting to play against him. He was outstanding at poker and crap games. According to Lonnie Lee, who watched Bob at the craps table, the man could spread money throughout a craps table and win like a painter creating a masterpiece. In Bob's world, he was second to none, but everyone with money liked to play him. Bob also liked to bet on sporting events and was an expert at picking the right odds on a game or race.

Not all of Bob's friends or acquaintances were people who gambled against him. Harold Haddan, an acquaintance, would mention Bob periodically during family trips down memory lane. He remembered Bob constantly bringing in pictures of celebrities he knew to be enlarged and copied. Harold respected Bob by reputation but also enjoyed him as a customer who paid in cash and always had a good story to tell. Like Harold, Bob was short and stocky. Both men also liked Native American jewelry with large turquoise stones.

Bob liked to bet on events; some were trivial, and others much larger. On one occasion, the Coffeyville City

Commission was about to vote on a controversial city matter. There had been much discussion on the subject, and most of the local citizens were anticipating a split vote. Most people knew at the time that one commissioner tended to vote against the majority and relied on his personal convictions of what was right or wrong. Prior to the commission meeting, he had lunch with local businessmen Perl Schmid and Bob Pratt. Schmid and Pratt knew his political sentiments and attempted to intimidate him into voting the way they preferred. After about 15 minutes of listening to their browbeating, the commissioner left the table. He later learned that Bob, who was having lunch nearby, went to Schmid and Pratt, pulled out a large wad of money and offered to bet on his vote. The two quietly declined.

Even though Southeast Kansas and Northeast Oklahoma, including Tulsa, took a major step back with the economic downturn that was hitting everyone by 1983, Bob continued his gambling events at home. By this time, all gambling above the supper club had stopped, and only Bingo was offered in the building behind it. Steve Born, a young man in the early 70s used to work at the Bingo parlor once commented that the cigarette smoke was so thick, he could barely see the bingo numbers to call. Pet and Kelly's café had turned into a bar and was showing its age. One Sunday in the early 80s, Lonnie Lee remembers going to the café with a friend to purchase a six-pack of beer. The place was dark and dingy, with patrons obviously not happy about two men who appeared to be strangers entering the place. Although more than capable of handling the unhappy patrons, Lonnie chose to avoid a confrontation and left the place after the purchase. Other than the club and Bones Café, there was essentially nothing else in Southtown. The town's main claim to fame now resided in its location as a bedroom community and haven for former Coffeyville residents who hated Kansas vehicle tax and tag fees. But, despite the current economy and state of Southtown, Bob continued to flourish. His gambling events always attracted plenty of customers and eventual losers. Bob prospered to the point he started investing in cattle for his ranch. He also built a large metal storage building on the property to his house, his large collection of classic cars. Bob participated in a mid-80s Coffeyville Fair and Rodeo parade and drove the rodeo queen contestant in a restored 1946 Ford convertible. Bob was driving, wearing one of his fancy cowboy hats.

CHAPTER 10
END OF AN ERA

As the 80sprogressed, Bob's Health declined. He had been a diabetic for years, and the disease was starting to take its toll. Despite his health problems, he continued to hold his gambling events but at a much slower pace. By this time in his life, Bob was very wealthy, purchasing his ranch with cash. When Bob's daughter was married in 1987, Bob went "all out" financially with a beautiful ceremony and reception. He hired Haddan Studio to photograph the wedding and purchased his most expensive package with cash. It would be Bob's last major event. On January 7, 1991, Bob succumbed to his illness and quietly passed away. There was no one in Coffeyville or Southtown to replace him.

SOUTHTOWN TODAY

Like its neighbor to the north, Southtown today is only a pale shadow of itself. In 2005, Bones Café closed, leaving only the supper club to serve food. Unfortunately, it was starting to show its age. Pete and Kelly's Bar eventually closed, and Southtown was without a bar. Local businessman Jesse Butcher had taken a small portion of the abandoned theater and turned it into a convenience store. By 2000, it was gone, and 20 years later, the theater was demolished.

When Bob passed away, his motel had already been sold and turned into low-end apartments. By 2000, it too had been demolished and turned into a large convenience store and truck stop called "The Woodshed." Also gone were the old post office building and former grocery store location. They were replaced by a building constructed by Welch State Bank.

Today, Southtown is a deteriorating community with only a little hope of rejuvenating. In 2008, The Cherokee Tribe built a small casino south of town where Tommy's old landing strip was located. The Southern Supper Club closed in 2017, leaving Southtown without a restaurant. According to local gossip, the club has been purchased by the Cherokee Tribe who plan to demolish the building and construct a fitness center. If a person looks at Southtown's Facebook page, one will think that the town is slowly becoming a Cherokee Tribe community. Hopefully their investment can turn the town around and make it prosperous again.

As for Southtown and its notorious past, the history of this community's beginning and sordid reputation diminishes with each passing year.

EPILOGUE

The reader will notice that, at times, this book has discussed the skeletons of Southtown's northern neighbor, Coffeyville. Even though the focus has always been Southtown, it is impossible not to mention Coffeyville. The two communities were so close geographically it was hard to mention one side of the border without discussing the other. In a way, both were co-dependent when it came to liquor and gambling. What happened in one town eventually would affect the other. The economic downturn that started in Coffeyville 50 years ago has now turned it into a town that is a pale shadow of its former self. The economic depression eventually went south of the state line, and it, too, hit Southtown hard. What a person will find today are two very rough-looking communities that might have been something special years ago. Coffeyville, with few industries and jobs that require skilled employees, has mostly become a dangerous town with a large percentage of its population on public assistance. A major flood in 2007 wiped out almost a fourth of the town and displaced almost as many residents. The downtown core is mostly a place that consists of poorly kept buildings and a handful of businesses. There are several restaurants there that have small bars but nothing more. Residents who want to eat at a fine dining establishment usually travel to Independence, Bartlesville, or Tulsa.

As for Southtown, the small Cherokee Tribe Casino is still in business. It consists mainly of slot machines and a small casual café. The Southtown Facebook page is usually filled with Cherokee events.

At this point in history, it will be hard to forecast what will eventually happen to Southtown and Coffeyville. Maybe they will recover, but if Bob was betting on the odds of that happening, the author believes he would be betting against it.

BIBLIOGRAPHY

GOVERNMENT DOCUMENTS

FBI Report on Bremer Kidnapping, October 31, 1936

BOOKS

The Encyclopedia of Kidnappings, Michael Newton, Author

DOCUMENTARIES

Tulsa Burning, the 1921 Race Massacre, 2021 television documentary

NEWSPAPER ARTICLES

1. Coffeyville Journal, September 15, 1953
2. Baxter Springs News, December 9, 1915
3. Ada Evening News, August 19, 1929
4. Ada Evening News, June 12, 1936
5. Ada Evening News, June 1, 1937
6. Miami Oklahoma Daily News Record, January 15, 1932
7. Miami Oklahoma Daily News Record, February 12, 1936
8. Miami Oklahoma Daily News Record, May 30, 1937
9. Miami, Oklahoma Daily News Record, January 16, 1940
10. Miami Oklahoma Daily News Record, March 8, 1940
11. Lawrence Daily Journal-World, August 20, 1934

12. Iola Register, November 26, 1934
13. Hutchinson News, March 15, 1934
14. Sedalia Capitol, January 5, 1932
15. Joplin News Herald, October 23, 1934
16. South Coffeyville Times, July 2, 1909
17. South Coffeyville Times, October 1, 1909
18. Lenapah Post, February 11, 1916
19. Lenapah Post, September 28, 1917
20. Nowata Daily Star, August 20, 1924
21. Nowata Daily Star, January 19, 1925
22. Nowata Daily Star, February 19, 1925
23. Nowata Daily Star, January 17, 1928
24. Nowata Daily Star, April 13, 1928
25. Nowata Daily Star, April 16, 1928
26. Nowata Daily Star, December 19, 1929
27. Nowata Daily Star, August 30, 1929
28. Nowata Daily Star, September 15, 1929
29. Nowata Daily Star, March 11, 1929
30. Nowata Daily Star, April 29, 1930
31. Nowata Daily Star, June 28, 1931
32. Nowata Daily Star, March 20, 1934
33. Nowata Daily Star, January 22-23, 1941
34. Nowata Daily Star, February 25, 1942
35. Nowata Daily Star, November 17, 1947
36. Nowata Daily Star, January 31, 1947
37. Nowata Daily Star, December 4, 1951
38. Nowata Daily Star, December 10, 1951
39. Parsons Sun, May 6, 1937
40. Parsons Sun, September 1, 1942
41. Manhattan Kansas Mercury, August 19, 1929
42. Wichita Beacon, November 20, 1935

43. Manhattan Kansas The Morning Chronicle, April 2, 1939
44. Coffeyville Daily Dawn, August 20, 1924
45. Vinita Daily Journal, March 23, 1943
46. Bartlesville Examiner-Enterprise, January 9, 1924
47. Bartlesville Examiner-Enterprise, March 11, 1930
48. Tulsa World, June 14, 1929
49. Tulsa World, January 3, 1930
50. Tulsa Daily Legal News, July 12, 1928
51. Tulsa Daily Legal News, August 16, 1928
52. Tulsa Tribune, April 12, 1928
53. Craig Oklahoma County Gazette, March 22, 1928
54. Shawnee Oklahoma Evening Star, May 22, 1931

REFLECTIONS AND COMMENTS FROM DECEASED INDIVIDUALS

1. Newton R Haddan, deceased 1978
2. Harold P Haddan Sr, deceased 1987
3. Patricia Ann Haddan, deceased 2013
4. Damon Wilbern, deceased 2019
5. Otto Ivey, former Coffeyville Police Chief, deceased
6. Allan Flowers, former Coffeyville Police Chief, deceased
7. Bill Clairborne, former Coffeyville Interim City Manager, deceased 1984
8. Earlene Clairborne, former Coffeyville community leader, deceased
9. Glenn Welch, former Coffeyville Police Major, deceased
10. Barbara Homer, former Coffeyville Assistant City Clerk, deceased 2023

11. Russell Cartwright, retired Coffeyville USD 445 Principal, Cleveland Elementary School, deceased
12. Arthur Treece, former Mayor of Coffeyville, deceased
13. Bob Jones, form South Coffeyville resident and Coffeyville City Commissioner, deceased

INDIVIDUALS WHO CONTRIBUTED INFORMATION FOR THIS BOOK

1. Lonnie Lee, former South Coffeyville and Coffeyville resident
2. George Elliot, current South Coffeyville resident
3. Debbie Lee, current South Coffeyville resident
4. Steve Garner, current Coffeyville resident
5. Bobby Owen, former Coffeyville resident
6. Mike Reister, former South Coffeyville resident
7. Kd Meek, Current Coffeyville resident
8. Debby Brown, former Coffeyville resident
9. Charles Vest, Current Coffeyville resident
10. Judith Collins Ross, former Coffeyville resident
11. Ed and Marilyn Todd, Current Coffeyville residents
12. Steve Born, former Coffeyville resident